Soldier's SECRET

The Story *of* Deborah Sampson

Soldier's SECRET

The Story of
Deborah Sampson

Sheila Solomon Klass

Christy Ottaviano Books
Henry Holt & Company
NEW YORK

Henry Holt and Company, LLC
Publishers since 1866
175 Fifth Avenue
New York, New York 10010
www.HenryHoltKids.com

Library of Congress Cataloging-in-Publication Data
Klass, Sheila Solomon.
Soldier's secret : the story of Deborah Sampson / Sheila Solomon Klass.—1st ed.
p. cm.
"Christy Ottaviano books."
Summary: During the Revolutionary War, a young woman named Deborah Sampson
disguises herself as a man in order to serve in the Continental Army.
ISBN-13: 978-0-8050-8200-5 / ISBN-10: 0-8050-8200-X
1. Gannett, Deborah Sampson, 1760–1827—Juvenile fiction.
2. United States—History—Revolution, 1775–1783—Juvenile fiction.
[1. Gannett, Deborah Sampson, 1760–1827—Fiction.
2. United States—History—Revolution, 1775–1783—Fiction.
3. Disguise—Fiction. 4. Sex role—Fiction. 5. Soldiers—Fiction.] I. Title.
PZ7.K67814So 2009 [Fic]—dc22 2008036783

First edition—2009 / Designed by Meredith Pratt
Portrait of Deborah Sampson on title page: courtesy of
the *Canton Journal Newspaper* and the Canton Historical Society.
Printed in the United States of America on acid-free paper. ∞

1 3 5 7 9 10 8 6 4 2

For Gabriel Julian and Madeleine Leta,
and for Anatol Elvis,
who introduced me to Deborah Sampson

Soldier's SECRET

The Story of Deborah Sampson

1. *The Smock-faced Boy*

"He's dead." The nurse's voice rang out loud and clear, indicating that she felt no further need to whisper. Then she slipped into the chaplain's solemn role for a moment and spoke more gently. "Rest in peace, Robert Shurtliff."

"Amen," the two orderlies responded.

"All right, gentlemen"—immediately, she was businesslike and brusque again—"let's clean up."

There followed a fearful clatter of instruments and bottles and tin basins.

Indeed, the corpse was not dead.

The corpse was me, and I was terrified.

Their voices came to me unevenly as echoes quivering over a long distance. These medics had done all they could possibly do, inspecting and pummeling me as they tried to revive me, as they sought a pulse, a heartbeat, any small sign of life. They'd given up after working for what seemed like hours once the plague cart, which carried the sick of Philadelphia to this almshouse converted to an army hospital, delivered me tied up in an old army blanket.

"Puking black and burning with a fever for four days," Mike O'Connor, the driver, reported. He was a bluff, red-faced, elderly man, with the resounding voice of a town crier. The nurse heard him, but, fortunately, the others around me were too sick themselves to listen.

He was eager to hand me over but had to wait while the orderlies cleared a body from a pallet.

"This soldier wouldn't go near a hospital, but when his skin turned yellow—well—the other men in his tent decided that the British couldn't kill him, but this fever might. So they wrapped him up and gave him to me."

The nurse's fingers searched for my pulse.

Finding that there was not a clean sheet left, the orderlies laid me on the bare, stained, straw mattress.

"They should have sent him when they first saw the jaundice," the nurse complained. "We've posted warnings everywhere. Soldiers are supposed to obey orders. Why did they wait so long?"

"Because," Mike said, "this lad's stubborn as a mule. They tried but he just wouldn't go. He swore to them that his folks' skin always colored this way when they were sick, and it was a natural thing."

"Pshaw!" The nurse dismissed that idea. "They should have forced him to come."

"Maybe he'll still make it," Mike said hopefully. "According to his mates, he fights like a tiger though he looks a bit of a sissy."

I could have done without that last bit of opinion, but it hardly mattered in this chaos, this hot stinking dispensary.

"I can't breathe in here," Mike complained, fanning his face with his cap. "'Tis truly like the plagues in the Bible." He coughed hard in the dense musk that came of medicines, blood and urine and vomit and human waste.

Men on cots were crammed side by side into every possible space. I lay below them on the floor in one of the rows of aligned mats covering the walking areas. The attendants had to tiptoe around the edges. Some of the sick slept; others groaned or cursed madly. One or two managed to stagger to their feet, turning into ghastly bandaged dancers toeing their way about until they were recaptured by orderlies. Most patients were bedridden and inert. Once in a while, a sleeper would wail pitifully for a mother or wife, for a missing leg or a lost sense.

Next to me lay a freckled, carrot-topped lad who couldn't have been more than fifteen, a black cloth sealing his eyes as if he were "It" in an interrupted game of blindman's buff. "I can't see, Mother," he whispered over and over, his open hands imploring. "Who will care for the chicks if I can't see?"

"You *will* see, Patrick, darlin'," the nurse comforted him. "You must rest now. I promise, you *will* see."

The boy turned and suddenly reached out to clutch Mike's shin. "Help me to see," he begged.

The nurse gently extricated the cartman's leg. "Step round over here, Mike. Give me the information on this soldier, then you can go."

"R-O-B-E-R-T S-H-U-R-T-L-I-F-F. Fourth Massachusetts Regiment, Light Infantry. Rangers under Captain Webb."

She recorded it. "Age?"

"Eighteen."

"Eighteen? A smock-faced lad," she said as she made her notes. "With that flaxen hair and no beard on his cheeks, he is more like sixteen."

The driver was coughing again. He pulled at his collar.

"Mike, I've kept you too long. Time to go and collect some more."

Driven by a Christian impulse, Mike lingered a moment longer to kneel beside me and whisper, "Goodbye, Bobby Shurtliff. God be with you."

His parting words rippled away from me as if carried by waves under water, the sounds growing fainter as the plunge deepened. My eyes followed Mike's macabre exit dance, first around Patrick and then around the other bodies and bedding and bedpans, the only path out of this charnel house. He leaned forth as if into the wind in his eagerness to be out of there. Though he did his driver's job responsibly, he surely did not relish his deliveries.

The nurse glanced over at Patrick, who was quiet now, and then at me. "A war fought by younger brothers and striplings," she muttered resentfully.

With gentle fingers, she repeatedly sought a pulse at my wrist till at last she sighed, pressed my eyelids closed, and pulled up the winding sheet. "We're done here," she said. "Notify Matron Parker and call the undertakers. I've got to make rounds."

On the spur came two hardened gravediggers to arrange for the burial.

I, though fully conscious, could not speak and did my best not to move. First and most immediate, each ghoul took hold of one of my boots and tugged so violently that I was sure they were trying to yank off my feet.

Then the grisly clowns began at once to quarrel.

"He will have no need for leather boots where he's goin', Pete," the first hoarse jocular voice decided.

To which there was a cackle of agreement. "You're right, Georgie. No need for them in potter's field."

"I'll have the boots then. They'll just fit me, for I'm tall as he is."

"Boots! You're wearin' the boots of the last bloke," Pete protested. "You've only got two feet. I can trade these—I'll get a good price for 'em."

"You take the britches," George rejoined.

"Britches don't bring much. Let's toss for it," the other scoundrel suggested, and in a moment he'd won the toss and claimed the boots.

"Well, let's see what other worldly goods 'e's got," the loser grumbled.

Quickly, they pulled the cover sheet off me so that

they could divest my body of its valuables. My great terror was that in the next moment they would strip off my breeches and thus reveal to the world what was private. I lay rigid.

"Wait!" The matron arrived and took command. She was old and sharp, and she thwarted them and saved me. She crouched down low and bent close, and then, making a horn with her hand over her mouth, she called as loudly as if she were signaling in the Alps, "Yoo-hoo, Robert Shurtliff, can you hear me?"

I needed to be left for dead.

I had no idea whether my rigid pose fooled her.

Again, in a voice truly loud enough to summon goats or, indeed, raise the dead, she roared, "Robert Shurtliff!" Then, again, she waited.

Surely she would now declare me dead and turn away.

Lying prostrate and holding my breath was good practice for being buried alive, a terrible fate but preferable to being discovered.

"Matron, this one's a corpse if I ever saw one," affirmed the boots-fancier enthusiastically.

"The poor sod's 'ad it," the other ruffian agreed. "Let's get on with the buryin' before he rots here and spreads the fever."

"I need to see your diploma before you practice medicine here," she snapped. "Be quiet so I can judge."

Waiting for her to declare me dead, I was agonized by the effort it took to control my weakened body. I was further disheartened by this indomitable woman. Why would she not believe her eyes? Why would she not accept defeat?

Give up and go away, I willed silently. I'm dead.

Holding my breath proved a mistake, for I suddenly gagged and a paroxysm seized my body.

The matron started. "Hark! He is still alive." She set her ear to my chest.

I could no longer suppress my heavy breathing.

"Dear Lord," she murmured, thankfully. "Yes, he is alive."

Rising now, she turned to face the undertakers, directing her fierce anger at the boot-holder. "Soldiers are to be buried with dignity, not robbed or stripped. Put those boots down and give me your billets."

There were whimpers of protest. "'E looked dead to me and already wearin' wings. 'E had no need of boots."

"Go, you two rascals, or I shall have you both court-martialed for grave robbing."

As they stumbled out, she summoned the sentry. "Fetch me Dr. Binney at once. One of our cadavers has risen from the dead!"

Her triumphant cry heralded my doom. Next there would be discovery and public ignominy. The nurse had closed my eyes and now I kept them sealed in despair, and I did my best not to listen to what was being said about me, for there was nothing I could do to save myself. Therefore I did not see the doctor with the distinguished goatee enter, consult with the nurse, and kneel down at once.

He thrust his hand inside my military jacket, feeling for a pulse. "Yes! There may be something!" he exclaimed softly. "Indeed—there *is* definitely something!"

His examination was hampered by the undergarment I had fashioned: a firm linen inner cloth, shoulders to waist and buckled in the back. It was a contrivance that tightly bound my chest, compressing all and blocking the doctor's fingers.

In a single motion of impatience, Dr. Binney lunged forward and ripped the cloth in two.

Then he freely inserted his hand. First there was an instant gasp of recognition, followed by a long silence once his fingertips truly identified what they'd brushed against. Breasts.

"Incredible!" He covered up my bare chest hastily.

I kept my eyes shut tight because my shame was so immense. Nothing but disgrace and humiliation could come upon me now. What would they find?

A young woman disguised as a man.

A young woman who had run away from home.

A Christian female clad in a man's clothing.

A soldier in the Continental army who had lied at the swearing-in. Who had slept in the barracks among men. Who had managed this deception for more than a year and a half.

Whatever my good intentions, my noble charade would be read as folly, as stubbornness, as boldness—as madness.

My tentmates and Mike had saved my life by bringing me to this hospital, and thus unwittingly exposed me to hideous dishonor, such as few women in the colonies had ever known.

"Rest in peace." Piously, the nurse had pronounced me dead. Ah, would that it were so. For only in death would I be at peace.

*　　*　　*

The doctor, distracted, was silent. He remained kneeling beside me.

"Dr. Binney?" inquired Matron Parker.

"This patient is most certainly alive," Dr. Binney declared resolutely, and he now hurried to take from his bag a small flask and administer a good dose of brandy, forcing it into my closed mouth and spilling it freely down my chin.

"Praise God," the good woman whispered. "It's a miracle."

"More than you know," the doctor muttered, a certain irony in his tone.

He performed a quick, cursory examination. "This soldier is very sick—a rare malady. He will die in this crowded place; he must be moved at once and sequestered. This is a most curious case. I shall attend him in my own home, where Mistress Binney herself will do the supervising. Isolation and privacy are crucial in this instance."

"In your own home, Doctor?" Matron Parker was clearly surprised. "You have never once before—all during this long war—"

"Matron Parker," he started very softly but firmly, "I must rely on your discretion as I always have in the past.

This case is extraordinary. I have never encountered one like it in my career. I trust you to care for him now till I take him away, and once he is gone you will forget that he exists."

"Yes, Doctor." Matron Parker respectfully accepted his judgment. "I shall follow your orders exactly. Private Shurtliff is lucky that he was brought here to you."

"Lucky? Hmmm. I'll grant that he's had extraordinary luck, if we discount the fact that he is mortally ill."

This doctor knew!

For the first time, a *man* knew my secret. If it disgusted him or horrified him or outraged him, he kept it to himself. He did not say a word about it. He went right on treating Robert Shurtliff.

My thoughts were filled with gratitude: You, sir, are an amazingly kind man. Because I am very ill and mute, you will try to help me recover before you turn me in, as is your duty. I will be sent to prison. Since I am now on my deathbed, that is hardly of consequence. It will simply come down to the name on the toe tag of a corpse. What matter is it if I be buried as Robert Shurtliff?

The doctor immediately began to prescribe medicines

and poultices. He sent the matron off to commandeer a bed so that they could raise me from the floor.

Before she returned, he bent down and spoke close to my ear. "Blink twice rapidly if you understand me."

I did as told.

"I believe you have a secret. Blink if that is so."

He watched closely.

"It is safe with me. If you can speak, say your name."

There was silence.

"Illness and shock have deprived you of words. Should your voice return, do not use it or all is lost. I shall give it out that you are mute and need special care.

"Blink if you understand me."

I complied.

"Perfect!" he said softly. "Now we are medical co-conspirators." And he rose.

When Matron Parker returned with an orderly, the doctor informed them, "The patient is mute from the illness."

"We must remove his soiled gar—" the matron started, but the doctor stopped her. "No. Let him rest. He is too feeble to be hastily handled here. A bed gown over what he's wearing will cover him for now. In my home he will be cleaned up and all his contagious clothing fumigated."

The doctor stayed on just long enough to supervise a careful transfer of me to the bed. "I shall notify my wife at once to send our carriage as conveyance," he told the matron. "Dispatch the patient to my house just as he is, the sooner the better. Till then keep him absolutely isolated."

Hastily, he took his leave.

"The doctor has probably recognized some rare dangerous ailment," Matron Parker confided to her aide. "He is very knowledgeable about such things."

Within an hour I was bundled into Dr. Binney's private chaise and driven to his home, where his cordial wife was waiting. "Welcome," Mistress Binney called from a safe distance as she supervised the coachman and the maid, who together conveyed me inside and upstairs. "You will recover quickly here," she called after me. "You must look upon our home as yours."

Installed alone in a vast, book-lined room at the top of the house, I was so weak and feverish that once in bed I immediately abandoned consciousness for sleep. For several days I mostly slept and swallowed food and drink, only feverishly aware of the activities around me; the coachman helping the doctor change the bed linen, the doctor attending me periodically with medicines and compresses or examining me. These two attendants were like gentle shadows spoon-feeding me and applying cool compresses to my burning brow. They plied me ceaselessly with chilled drinks, for even in my stupor I was ravaged by the fever's thirst.

When I finally truly awoke, I found myself washed and freshly clad. The fever had broken. I lay in this handsome attic room, apparently the doctor's study, for the books on the shelves were huge volumes, probably medical texts. On opposite walls facing each other, two human skeletons dangled from hooks.

I did not care much for these roommates. Mind, I am not afraid of skeletons; still, they offer no conversation and are not pretty sights. But I had little choice. Pete and George I christened them. "You see what happens to grave robbers," I instructed them silently. "Now, *you* have little use for boots. And you will surely never sprout wings."

Days had passed—I knew not how many—but I was now alert. And alone. I was, of course, happy to be alive, and then quickly despondent. Unable to decipher the doctor's motives, I feared the worst. Why was he protecting my secret? Why had he not turned me over to the military?

I was completely at his mercy. Had he told his wife of my situation? How could he have explained it? There on the luncheon tray alongside the crockery was a lovely red rose. Did Mistress Binney know I was female? Into my head came vague recollections of swallowing savory soups and smooth creamy puddings, which she must have prepared. What did she think? A small glass vase on the night table contained other short-stemmed blossoms, two tulips, a lily, and a sprig of rosemary. Surely they were gifts from earlier meal trays, kind tokens from the lady of the house. But I, myself, had not been visited. Of course, there were young daughters—their hushed laughter drifted up and was a sweet sound—and they had to be shielded from the disease.

Still—I was powerless, an unprotected young woman. Was he going to take advantage of my desperate situation? Surely not. I'd overheard Matron Parker say that he was a man of integrity and character, a fine doctor, and he had, indeed, saved my life.

But I was isolated and had no voice. If anything untoward should happen, who would believe me? I well knew that a young woman alone in the world was vulnerable and had to be constantly on guard. I had known this, for I had been a child on my own.

In a kind of hysterical frenzy, my eyes cast about desperately for some means of self-defense. A sharply pointed metal letter-opener lay upon his neat desk, and I immediately reached for it and concealed it inside my pillow slip.

When he came upstairs and glanced round the room, of course he missed it immediately. "My letter-opener is absent from my desk, Private Shurtliff. And I surmise that it has not absented itself. You must have it, though you will have no need for it unless you are expecting letters. I hope it is not concealed on your person for it is dangerously sharp. May I have it back?"

Meekly, I retrieved it and returned it to his hands.

"Well, then . . ." He placed it on the desk. "Private Shurtliff, my interest in you is purely clinical. I am a happily married man."

He smiled, pausing long that I might absorb his words.

"I am intrigued by your situation. I will make a bargain with you. I have taken a great risk to aid you, out of sympathy and curiosity—and because I have an intimation that you will one day be my most famous, or, perhaps, most notorious patient. Therefore, I need to know your story. You have no voice, and our time is limited. I need to have the particulars of the singular life that brought you here."

I felt my face grow warm.

"What?" He scrutinized me closely. "You blush that your doctor would learn about how you have lived! Are you ashamed of your life?"

I denied it with an emphatic shake of my head.

"With a show of fingers, tell me how many months you have been in the army."

I flashed the fingers of my left hand thrice and then extended two fingers more.

"That long!" he exclaimed in astonishment. Then he cautioned me softly. "When your voice returns, you must not speak on this subject to anyone. Particularly to my wife, who would be compromised by hearing such information. I am an army doctor bound by my oath. You are in our home illegally."

He tugged at his small beard. "Yet I must know all: how you conceived this extraordinary deception; how, without privacy, you handled bathing, dressing, nature's calls, a woman's monthlies; what you thought and planned and hoped. You have lived a natural impossibility. For a doctor such information is a treasure. So, as a doctor, I need to know how you managed this!" He paused. "Blink to indicate you understand."

I did.

"Good. You would have died in that hospital. The care here will be the best I can offer. I will attend you till you are recovered, but when your voice returns *I* do not wish to *hear* your secrets either."

How then . . . ? My puzzlement must have shown on my face.

He put up his hand to indicate he had not finished. "Can you read and write? Signal."

I blinked.

Taking a writing tablet from a drawer, he set it along with a quill and ink pot on the desktop. "Very well. Now you must tell your story to save your own life." To himself he muttered, "Like Scheherazade."

I took up the pen and wrote:

I loved those tales. "Aladdin" was my favorite.

Dr. Binney, reading my words, was clearly astonished. "*You* have read *A Thousand and One Nights*?"

I nodded, and wrote:

My French-speaking grandmother introduced me to them. Though her favorite story was a true one—about Joan of Arc.

The doctor smiled. Perhaps he, too, admired Joan of Arc. I think he was reassured by my literacy that the great risk he was taking was worthwhile. Readers respect one another, and I was a reader. I was no ordinary country soldier.

"See here—there is no need to be embarrassed or uncomfortable. I am a Bostonian and a sophisticated man, a student of human nature as well as a doctor. No truth will shock me.

"Write how this strange situation came to pass. Tell of your childhood and family, of how you lived and how you managed. Leave *nothing* out. It will be difficult for you to record such things, but the smallest and most private detail will be useful. When a doctor charts a case, he needs an accurate history."

I nodded to show I understood.

"Nothing you confide will be revealed to anyone else, I promise. I will consider all your information and weigh it carefully before I decide what to do when I discharge you.

"You will keep the written pages in the locked drawer of this desk. Here, take this." He handed over a tiny silver key.

"You have been here just a week," he said. "I estimate

you will need a full month more to be completely recovered. Now, please write your true name on the first sheet so I may know that much." He dipped the pen, then handed it to me with the tablet.

Deborah Sampson, I wrote.

My handwriting was shaky. I did not stop there:

Please bring a Bible so that I may begin at once.

He read the request, looked at me curiously, and ripped the page into bits. Then he vanished, to return moments later with a worn family Bible, which I pressed to my lips, for I am a true Christian.

Once he left, I summoned enough energy to sit up and inscribe an epigraph in bold capital letters:

I PLEDGE ON THIS HOLY BIBLE THAT WHAT I WRITE IS MY TRUE HISTORY.

I signed it and would have written more but fatigue and excitement proved me faint. Locking it away, I collapsed into a healing sleep.

In the following days, I proceeded, first a sentence or two at a time, then several that grew into paragraphs, which became pages. The story I had so long contained silently spilled out of me like milk from an upended jug.

2. A Give-away Child

You ask: How did I first come to such a bold idea? How did I dare to enlist?

Only the Lord knows. I cannot say with surety.

I knew that earlier in these colonies women were imprisoned as witches and some were hanged. For lesser crimes they were made to stand upon the gallows or were put in the stocks so that the good citizens could gape and jeer and shake their fingers.

No, I was not ignorant of history.

In the year 1778, in the earlier days of this War of Independence, just before my eighteenth birthday I overheard a drunk veteran in Sproat's Inn entertain the other citizens by telling of a maiden named Nancy Bailey in Elizabethtown, New Jersey, who had that week been discovered in army breeches! How the man laughed as he told his tale. She had been in the army only a few days and had forgotten herself and curtseyed while setting a beer tankard on the table for her commanding officer. The general there sentenced her to have her bodice ripped and to be lashed as she ran the gauntlet while the drums beat the whore's march.

Poor lass. Curtseying becomes routine for polite maidens, like blinking. I didn't forget the story.

Of one thing I am certain: I never wanted to be a boy *or* a man. I was content in my femininity. What I always wanted was to be *the equal* of any boy. Tell me if that is a sin.

Perhaps, for me, the strange notion was first born with my French grandmother, Bathsheba Bradford, who read marvelous adventure tales to me when I was a babe. Best of all, Grandmother recited the *true* story of Joan of Arc, who early heard holy voices calling her to save her land. As a child, I thought often of this Maid of Orleans, whose army defeated the British and drove them out of France. I pictured her clad in breeches marching amidst her soldiers, her tumbled hair a blaze of brilliant light.

Joan, who would answer only to God, was cruelly betrayed. Men of God tied her to a stake and burned her. How could churchmen do that? I wept for Joan till my pillow was soaked. When Ma questioned me and I explained, she had no patience. "That was more than three hundred years ago, silly goose," she scolded. As if time mattered.

When I heard my own heavenly voice and recognized it at last, I understood. I, too, had a calling.

It is also possible that my imagination was excited by the adventure of my father's cousin, Captain Simeon Sampson. I was very young when I heard him tell of it.

"I was trapped," he had boasted. "The French captured me in that bitter French and Indian War. I escaped from my ship by dressing like a woman." He was a very large man and demonstrated how he folded pillows round for his bosom. Father and the other men hung on his every word admiring this ruse: how, in a bonnet and corsets and petticoats, he became a hero! His hands arced over his chest to show the plump breasts he'd made, and the men rocked with laughter.

"Cousin, can I be your cabin boy?" I asked at once.

He laughed at me, and when he had his breath back he explained, "You can never be a cabin boy, for you are a girl. Girls," he declared, "are made to be mothers and wives and to churn sweet butter."

That did not seem fair. He had become a hero for dressing like a woman! Nor did I like being mocked. Even worse, Father laughed right along with him. "My pretty little Yankee rose, a cabin boy!"

"The Maid of Orleans did not churn sweet butter," I retorted, and ran from the room, my face crimsoned by my boldness.

Perhaps I found my way through my own reading, for I am a great lover of books and tales both spoken and read. Reading, especially reading Shakespeare, held a lantern to my eager imagination.

I think that must be why our colonial fathers don't educate girls. The Bible is what we *must* read, if we're lucky enough to have mothers who teach us our letters. For our lives—birthing, cooking, spinning, sewing, planting, and child raising—the Bible suffices.

Our men, even the simple ones who can't tell which shoe goes on which foot, get to do the thinking and deciding about all the important things. Men handle all the property and all the money, even their wives' inheritances. My father was improvident, so we lost it all. Women own nothing. A wed couple is considered as a single person—the man makes the decisions.

We women are but shadows. What need have shadows

to read? I am a shadow who dared to read but not to speak her thoughts aloud. Even now, though I write them, I tremble and would not utter them. I secretly record them here for I have sworn this history shall be true. So be it.

Perhaps it was my reading Shakespeare's *Twelfth Night, or What You Will* that really planted the idea in my head. I thought the character Viola absolutely glorious, a shipwrecked girl, orphaned and alone, transforming herself and fooling everyone into believing she was a young man. Daily, as I sat weaving, spinning, making soap, I imagined her no less a girl for all of that. What courage!

> *"I am all the daughters of my father's house,*
> *And all the brothers too."*

These speculations get me nowhere. I cannot say why I did it but only tell what happened. And I am ahead of myself.

It is necessary to know the very beginning of my story in order to understand my plight.

I was a give-away child.

I was born in Plympton, Massachusetts Bay Colony, on December 17, 1760, and there I lived with my seven brothers and sisters. I come of good Puritan stock, a large Mayflower family spread throughout the colony.

Captain Miles Standish, John and Priscilla Alden, and William Bradford, the governor of Plymouth, were all forebears of mine, all good citizens and devout Congregationalists.

My father struggled to farm in Massachusetts. "A healthy weed grows for every seed he plants," Ma often noted tartly. He was, indeed, an inept farmer but a fond father, quite devoted to me. He loved to call me his Yankee rose.

"You favor me," he would note, priding in my fair hair, my deep blue eyes, and ivory skin. When tomboy pranks—racing, exploring, climbing—got me into trouble with Mother, he would defend me. "She's a spirited one is all," he'd say, "like me." That argument didn't do me much good with Ma, but I loved it anyway.

He liked to drink, Father did, and as the weeds grew and farming failed, his thirst increased as in a drought.

When I was five, Father decided to follow his dreams and seek his fortune in England. "Do not forget me, Yankee rose," he whispered into my ear late one night, then he ran away to sea and was lost forever.

I have hated England ever since.

Father drowned in a fearful storm, some said. Others snickered that he had just moved to another colony and taken another wife. Ma ordered us to forget him and never speak of him, for he had deserted us. How could I forget?

Had he not bade me *remember* him? So I spoke often of him, and before I was six years old, I was, alas, called willful and impertinent, and I was severely punished.

He was both friend and father, and he loved me. I missed him fiercely and believed he'd come back. I'd look out for him whenever travelers passed on the road and ask, "Have you not met my lost father, Jonathan Sampson?"

"Forget that foolishness," Mother scolded, but I never did. Often in the night I'd hear his voice whisper, "Do not forget me, Yankee rose," and I'd feel his breath in my ear.

Ma harkened only to Massachusetts, but Father heard the summons of the whole world. I certainly favored him.

After he left, Ma couldn't keep her children. She was poor and sick so she had to give us away. Out of eight, she gave away five, keeping only the younger ones with her once she was hired as a servant in Plympton. She was not a bad or uncaring mother, though I was never her Yankee rose. Her favorite child, her pride, had been Robert Shurtliff, her eldest, who'd died at the age of eight just before I was born.

She simply could not provide for us.

The other children went away obediently. Not me. "I won't go," I screeched, grasping the bedpost. "I have to stay here where we live, so Father can find me when he comes back."

"Of course you will go. I am your mother and I say so." Mother tried to pry me loose.

I dug my nails into the wood. "You can't make me. No one can make me."

"She is an impertinent child, and I fear she has a streak of disobedience," my mother said to Ruth Fuller, the elderly cousin who had come to take me home with her. "She is the only one of the children with whom I have these troubles."

This was a warning to my new guardian that I needed to be severely disciplined.

But Cousin Ruth proved to be wise and kind. "Perhaps she is just of strong and individual character," she guessed. "We do not expect that in girls but it sometimes occurs." Bending down, she whispered into my ear. "I know you love to hear stories. I shall teach you to read by yourself, and I have many wonderful books." She waited several minutes, then opened my willing fingers away from the bedpost.

I turned on my mother. "Father told me not to forget him, and I won't. But if you give me away now, I'm not yours anymore." I stamped my foot and shouted madly, "You are not my mother." I was very young and felt betrayed. "I have no mother!"

Thus I was passed around, as the children of indigents are, first to this elderly cousin Ruth Fuller, who lived in Middleborough, four miles away. I missed my family, but Miss Fuller gave me a room, and I had my own patchwork star quilt and soft feather bed. She was plump and jolly and liked children, although she had none of her own.

Cousin Ruth kept her word about teaching me. "You are my joy," she said many times as I learned my letters from a rhyming alphabet book. I started by memorizing:

> *In Adam's fall*
> *We sinned all.*

And went all the way up to:

> *Zaccheus, he*
> *Did climb the tree*
> *His Lord to see.*

Cousin Ruth owned many books besides the Bible. She taught me my catechism and how to read. Soon after my sixth birthday, I surprised her by reciting back the little verse she'd just read me.

> *Thirty days hath September,*
> *April, June, and November.*
> *All the rest have thirty-one*
> *Excepting February alone,*
> *Which hath but twenty-eight, in fine,*
> *Till Leap Year gives it twenty-nine.*

She hugged me and said, "Your name should rightly be Deborah Smart." She owned *The History of Little Goody Two-Shoes* and *Mother Goose Melodies*, which had lovely verses, and *Jack the Giant-Killer*. She was a wonderful reader and from her love of books came mine. I also learned from her how to bake bread and cookies. I was happy with Miss Fuller, until she got sick and died when I was eight years old.

No more Yankee rose.

No more Deborah Smart.

My childhood was over.

For I had no home, and the only person willing to give me my keep in exchange for "simple tasks" was a very old woman, Widow Thacher, in Middleborough. She was eighty and she couldn't do anything at all; "simple tasks" turned out to be simply *all* the household tasks, and, besides, I had to wash old Widow Thacher and cook the gruel. She couldn't even hold a spoon. I had to feed her like a little baby. Little babies are cute but she wasn't. When she wet or soiled herself, I had to clean her up just like an infant. It was hard.

I worked morning to night: making the fire, bringing in the wood, scrubbing the clothes, sweeping. Widow Thacher rocked all day in her rocker and mumbled only to God. In that gloomy, silent house, I missed the chatter of my brothers and sisters. I was tired all the time from the heavy work and terribly lonely. I comforted myself by talking to any living thing, a mouse or a woodcock or a bird flying by. Mostly I talked to myself, for there was no one else.

When Reverend Conant, the Congregationalist minister, came to call, I gave him peppermint tea and he bade me sit on the bench beside him. "How are you getting on?" he inquired, sipping his tea. On these periodic visits, he always asked the same question, without even looking at me or indicating interest.

I knew that the question simply required the polite

affirmative, "Well, sir." Children were hardly worth notice, indigent children even less than that, and no child had any right to complain.

This time, I did not say, "Well, sir." Instead, I dropped my head and snored so that he might guess my weariness and see how frail I was and how far gone the old lady was.

"How are you getting on, Deborah?" he asked, louder, through my false snores. I kept on snoring and did not even flutter my eyelashes. Perhaps it was wicked of me to deceive the minister, but I was desperate. Surely he smelled the Widow Thacher. I could. She needed to be changed.

Reverend Conant shook me by the shoulders. "Child, I am speaking to you."

"Oh! Oh!" I yawned mightily. "Sorry, Reverend, I am so weary. I must have fallen asleep."

He sniffed the foulness in the room. "Hmmm. I'll have to make new arrangements for you, Deborah," he promised, and he did.

Old Widow Thacher was sent, forthwith, to live with relatives. I, with my mother's written consent, was bound in indenture to Deacon Thomas and his family on their farm, two miles from Four Corners in Middle-borough, till I was eighteen years old.

Eighteen!

"You won't be alone, Deborah," Reverend Conant promised. "You'll be part of their family."

What he forgot to say was which part. You know which part? I was to be *the servant part* for the next ten years, as the family grew bigger and bigger. Deacon Thomas was a strict and rigorous elder of the church. Surely Reverend Conant and Mother chose him so that I would be thoroughly chastised and supervised. I often thought later, ruefully, that my snoring cost me dear, but I had little choice.

Mistress Thomas was a docile, motherly woman, greatly skilled at housewifery and completely ruled by the deacon. They already had four sons when I came, and two more were born afterward.

Indenture is just like slavery, only for a fixed time. I belonged to the Thomas family the same as if I were a cow. In fact, I was their chattel, which perfectly rhymes with *cattle*. All the Thomases had but one favorite form of address for me: "Deborah, do this. . . ."

"I will be *in loco parentis*," the deacon said importantly, rubbing his hands. "That is Latin for 'in place of your father.'"

Oh, no you won't, I thought. *Never!*

Once in a great while, my mother managed to come by and see me. Otherwise, she wrote me sometimes and sent messages with wayfarers passing through. She and the little ones were managing. She always had advice, much of it from Mr. Ben Franklin, whose *Almanack* she admired. I did not care for such letters warning me that "Lost time is never found again" or "He that goes a-borrowing goes a-sorrowing." I never had a minute's time to waste nor did I ever borrow, for I could not pay back. And no one would lend to me. Not one *motherly* letter did I ever receive. Why didn't she write about how much she loved or needed or missed me? I hoped and hoped for that. Why didn't she send along a sweet? She never remembered me with as much as a thimble on my birthday. That hurt me. I have always loved birthdays.

Indeed, I now had a place to live, good food to eat, and clothes to wear. In exchange I was nursemaid to the youngest Thomas boys; I diapered them, dressed them, fed them, told them stories, and played with them. I slept in the loft with the children, but I was not a child, I was a bound creature.

On rare occasions, I even went to the village school with the boys. More often, I had to beg to borrow their books secretly or ask them to tell me what they'd learned. "Why do you want to know so much?" they'd ask, thinking my questions strange. I honestly didn't know why I wanted to know. "Because God put it there to be known" was all I could answer.

Nature and the earth—the entire universe interested me. I asked questions about everything: the stars, the sun, the planets, faraway places.

I began to wonder about politics. I listened to the men grumble that "George is king and Oliver is judge." The Oliver family, owners of the iron foundry, also owned most else and ran Middleborough, including our church, where they had the best pew. The local farmers hated the Olivers just as much as they hated the wealthy, British-appointed officeholders in Boston who ran the colony. I heard all this and had a lot of questions. I had to bite my lip to keep from asking them.

I loved to wander on the roads and in the village and watch people and listen in on conversations. I did no harm, but this great interest I had in learning about impractical things unsettled folks, particularly my *in loco parentis.* "You have an odd mind, girl," he chided me, "an unwomanly mind."

"It is the mind the good Lord gave me, sir," I

responded. I learned to call on the good Lord frequently when the deacon and I differed. The good Lord was a powerful ally, the only one I had.

For ten years I lived with the deacon sharply watching my every move. He did not like me. He often spoke against "free spirits" that needed to be tamed.

I Good-Lorded the Deacon a lot. He could not object to my piety.

Besides caring for the young ones, I labored at every other task. I cleaned, cooked, carried water, swept, and brought in firewood. I learned to card wool, spin, and weave. The middle finger of my left hand grew stiff and malformed from all the woolwork. I fed livestock, I milked, I butchered, I churned and plowed and harvested. I could whittle and use wood tools. And I learned how to shoot and hunt.

I grew strong and healthy from this hard life. I was well muscled and much taller than any other young woman my age.

Then came those few strange days of the month when I had a womanly flow. The first time I bled, I was terrified. "Oh God, I know I am a sinner, but do stop me from bleeding," I prayed. This time God did not oblige, and the bleeding went on for a week. Finally, trembling with fright, for I knew this was some dreadful punishment, I sought out Mistress Thomas.

"There, there," she said calmly, "it is woman's burden, the legacy of Eve. We need to hold the color in your cheeks, for you are a woman now." She slapped me vigorously. "That will keep you rosy." She smiled and embraced me. From then on, she kindly supplied me with little cloths, which I was to wash privately each month. I was most grateful; I should surely have died of worry over the bleeding. My mother never thought to write to me and mention this condition at all, nor did I ever tell her I bled.

So, though I lived alongside six boys who treated me like just another boy, I never forgot I was a girl.

Deacon Thomas kept close watch. His eyes were always upon me. "What can that be in your apron pocket?" he would often inquire, his tongue curled in his cheek. "Surely not another book."

Though Deacon Thomas loved to read, he had strong misgivings about *my* reading. "You are always hammering upon some book," he reproached me. If he caught me writing, he'd grumble. "I wish you wouldn't spend so much time scrabbling over paper." He believed it was virtuous for a woman to admire learning in men. For her to want knowledge for herself was folly.

"Wasting your time, girl?" he would jibe. "Better be at your chores. Heed this tale from Governor Winthrop's journals," he bade me one day. He read from a book:

> There was an unfortunate young woman, who lost her understanding and reason because she had given herself wholly to reading and writing.
>
> If she had kept her place, if she had attended to household affairs and such things as belong to women and not gone out of her way and calling to meddle in such things as are proper for men, whose minds are stronger, she'd have kept her wits and the place God meant for her. She came to a tragic end.

"You want to beware of that folly," Deacon Thomas cautioned me. "You must attend to the womanly tasks for which you are fitted."

"Yes, sir," I said meekly, but, of course, I kept reading on the sly. Grandmother and Cousin Ruth had taught me that reading was a blessing, not a sin.

The deacon found fault with me endlessly as I grew older. "You must tie up those sinful blond locks," he would warn me. "That skirt allows your ankle to show."

Once he nearly rubbed the skin off my ruddy cheeks with a white cloth, for he suspected my high color. "There'll be no rouge in this house," he declared. There wasn't; the napkin came off clean. "'Tis the devil that puts such color there," he muttered.

He was too fond of repeating Governor Winthrop's cautionary tale. "You may remember . . ." he would start, and then I had to hear the whole story again. As though I could ever forget it.

When a tutor came to teach the older Thomas boys, I mourned, for I was, of course, excluded. I stopped eating and took to bed and was ill. Mistress Thomas, learning the cause of my melancholy, spoke to her husband for me. "If Deborah has finished her chores, then might she be allowed to sit and listen at lessons?"

"To what purpose?" He was not pleased with the suggestion.

"Why, then she could teach the younger boys and prepare them for their regular lessons."

The deacon was a thrifty man, and he saw frugality in this. He grudgingly gave me permission. "You will be allowed to sit in on the lessons if your tasks do not interfere."

I never let my tasks interfere. I became incredibly fast

at household chores, for I prized this schooling over all else I did. I could wash a floor or bring in wood or milk a cow in minutes. Sometimes I thought I saw surprise in the cows' dumb brown eyes when I squeezed their teats so speedily. "Sorry," I'd mumble, "got to squirt fast so I can be Deborah Smart." Lucky it didn't curdle the milk. Lucky the cows couldn't complain.

"You are very keen for a girl," the tutor once told me privately. "Indeed, even keener than any of the Thomas boys, though that seems impossible."

In the strongbox that is my heart, I have treasured that "keen" along with "Yankee rose" and "Deborah Smart"; these praises became my jewels.

I made sure my learning was useful to the family, by spending many hours reciting with the small children from my lessons, *always* where Deacon Thomas could hear us. He stopped reminding me of Governor Winthrop's sad tale of the learned madwoman. I did not miss that stupid story, which I never truly believed.

During tutoring we endlessly glossed Shakespeare's *Hamlet* and *King Lear,* then, one blessed afternoon, the tutor said, "Let us abandon the tragedies and take a lighter turn with Thalia, the muse of comedy." The Thomas boys cheered, and I did too (but silently, for I was mostly a listener to these lessons). To my joy, I was elected to read the part of Viola in *Twelfth Night, or What You Will.* Her wondrous concealment sang in my brain.

Bereft of family during all these years of my indenture, I had no girlfriends save one, Jennie, a Negro slave owned by Judge Oliver. Jennie was my age and pretty, the color of the heart of a black-eyed Susan. Sometimes we'd walk in the woods together and talk. Jennie was smart but could not read nor write. I offered to teach her but she was afraid. "Slaves aren't s'posed to read 'n write, Deb," she said, looking frightened. "The judge wouldn't like it."

"Well then, don't tell 'im."

Jennie just laughed merrily at the idea of keeping such a secret. She thought I was very bold.

She liked to hear stories about Noah and his ark and Moses in Egypt and Job. Joan of Arc made her weep. She listened to all my far-fetched dreams of wandering and having great adventures. Whenever I grumbled, she would tell me how lucky I was and what a good life I had.

"You live nice in a big farmhouse with the Thomases.

You eat their same food. They religious people and kind to you."

"But they're not my kin."

"Deborah, the judge *bought* me for money."

"Still, your mother didn't sign you away. You live with your own mother. I don't."

"But the judge can *sell* me—or us—like sheep or chickens anytime. He can *rent* me—like a plow—to other people."

"I am a bound girl to the Thomases till I am eighteen. That's like slavery."

"No, it's not, for then you'll be free. Nothing is like slavery! I will never, never, never be free. Never!" She was trembling with the horror of it.

"I know, Jen." I hugged her.

I did feel sad for Jennie. I truly did. But I was selfish and mostly feeling the pinch of my own shoe.

So I'd grumble on and on. "I wish I owned books, many books, so I could read to my heart's content."

"Oh, but you're such a good reader already. And you have a Bible. I wish I had a Bible. I wish I could read."

"Jennie, whatever you want to do, if it doesn't hurt

anyone or cause trouble, is fittin'. You learning to read wouldn't hurt the judge. Wouldn't hurt nobody."

"How you talk, Deb. How you talk. You have freedom comin'. That's why. Good thing you weren't born a slave. You'd make one terrible slave."

I almost answered "I would die," but I stopped just in time and said, "Amen to that." Jennie laughed. She was right. It was hard to be a give-away child, but it was much worse to be a slave, to believe you'd never get anything you wished for.

One day Jennie whispered to me, "Teach me to read the Bible, Deb." So we had secret lessons in the woods. I taught her her letters too. I wanted her to do lessons from the Thomas boys' copy of *The New England Primer*, but she was very stubborn and would read only "the direct words of God." She said the judge wouldn't mind that so much if he found out.

I liked being a teacher.

Often, on errands to the inn in Middleborough, where I delivered eggs and cheese, I listened to the men talk of politics and I read the *Boston Gazette* and other newspapers.

On December 17, 1773, my thirteenth birthday, I

went to the inn with two fresh cheeses and found an uproar there. "No taxation without representation," Mr. Sproat, the innkeeper, kept shouting merrily as he served the pints and quarts of ale. "Mind your p's and q's," he'd call as he chalked men's drinks on the slate. "Three hundred forty chests of tea in the harbor yesterday," he reported gleefully. "That's what I call a tea party. Wish I was there!"

"How'd they do it?" a traveler wanted to know. I was so glad he'd asked; it was my unspoken question. My business there was over but I lingered, even though I knew Deacon Thomas would scold me for my late return.

"They disguised themselves as Indians with lots of feathers and paint and just sneaked aboard those three British ships. People said Paul Revere and John Hancock were among them. No taxation without representation! Mind your p's and q's."

I left the inn dizzy with excitement and pleasure. The timing was perfect; the Boston Tea Party on the eve of my birthday was *my* birthday party as well. It had to mean something. It was a special celebration. It wasn't accidental. Nor was it to be forgotten.

The angry king of England marked that special tea party by sending many red-coated soldiers during the next years. Boston Harbor was closed because King George wanted to starve out the citizens of Boston until the tea was paid for. There was talk in the village of war. I listened carefully, never a part of the conversation, but I cared passionately.

Many months passed and then one night Paul Revere and William Dawes came galloping over the roads warning us, "The British are coming! The British are coming!" The redcoats were searching for hidden arms and gunpowder, and when they arrived in Concord and Lexington, more than fifty minutemen were waiting for them.

The war had started at last.

I lay awake in my bed for hours, my heart pounding, listening to the church bells tolling. They rang out: War, war, war! War, war, war!

And when I finally fell asleep I had a wondrous, terrifying dream.

On a calm and beautiful evening, I was running happily through the countryside. I stopped to rest on the summit of a hill. Suddenly the sky turned black and there was lightning and crashing thunder. The air filled with the stench of sulphur. The valley below became a raging sea in which ships, like the one on which my dear father died, were smashed by the waves against rocks. A hideous serpent, bright green with a black tongue, emerged and writhed toward me. The streets through which he passed were drenched in blood. I tried to scream for help but I was voiceless. Desperate, I ran home to escape from it.

I expected to be safe inside, but the beast was coiled there already in my room, its great green body taking up the whole space as it flicked its tongue wildly at me, its eyes balls of fire. I screamed, but no sound came.

A voice commanded me, "Arise, stand on your feet. Gird yourself and be strong." I jumped on my bed as the serpent moved to swallow me. Looking about for a weapon, I seized a log and attacked the monster. It turned and moved away as I pursued it, ducking its head as it tried to strike me with its studded tail.

It then turned into a fish divided into several sections bearing large gilt letters, which read: "The Rights of Man Are for All!" The fish fled into the street with me chasing it and beating it until it was broken into pieces on the ground. The monster re-formed into the shape of a raging bull and tried to gore me with its huge sharp horns, but I smashed him so hard with the log he turned into jelly. . . .

I awoke from this dream screaming, though there was nothing present to terrify me. I did not know what it meant. I was frightened by the vast darkness, the nothingness. I had neither mother nor father to comfort me. I was very alone and, of course, did not dare speak of my terror.

On the village green, I saw the boys and men training to be soldiers. They had to be ready to fight at a minute's notice, so they were called minutemen. I was a secret minutewoman. I practiced in my room late at night: I could jump out of bed, be dressed and ready so fast! If only . . . if only.

Mind your own business, Deb. War has not come for you. War is not for young women, I reminded myself sternly.

But the voice in the dream had commanded: "Arise, stand on your feet, gird yourself as you prepare to encounter your enemy."

In the darkness whenever I thought of the voice, I shivered deep under my quilt. I was neither brave nor free. I did not understand what was being asked of me.

Deacon Thomas came upon me in the barn reading *Common Sense,* Thomas Paine's thrilling pamphlet. "Common sense is what you lack," he said severely, smacking my face and wresting the pamphlet from my hand. "This is not fit reading for young women. A sensible girl would know that." He had this funny habit of wetting his lips, as if scolding me were delicious. "Politics"—he waggled his sharp-nailed forefinger under my nose—"are not your affair. You have too much free time. We must find you more tasks to keep you busy."

He locked up the pamphlet, but I read it in Sproat's public house when I next went on an errand. Then, on my way out, when no one was looking, I casually measured myself against the notch on the front of the tavern that established the height for Continental soldiers. I was five feet seven inches, well above the qualification, and I was still growing. After that, every time I visited Sproat's, if I could manage to do it unnoticed, I stopped to measure at the notch. Grow, girl, grow, I urged myself, and I did stretching exercises every night.

I kept saying to myself, Deborah, it's not your affair. But I wasn't really listening. I was watching soldiers drilling on the green. I was cheering for the new sign that went up outside Sproat's: SONS OF LIBERTY ENTER-TAINED HERE. I could not get the war out of my head, for it continued on and on. It went on so long that

Middleborough became divided, neighbor against neighbor, Loyalists against Patriots.

Judge Oliver, who loved the king and was Jennie's rich master, had to empty and close up his velvet-walled mansion and flee to England, away from his neighbors' wrath.

The war had already altered all of our lives.

3. A Masterless Woman

At last, I was free! In 1778, on reaching the glorious age of eighteen, I came to the end of my indenture. I was a *masterless woman!* Not only was I without a master, but I had neither father nor husband to confine me. I was independent and could earn my own keep. How many young women in the Massachusetts Bay Colony could so boast? Few, I warrant.

Imagine my joy!

"What will you do?" Deacon Thomas inquired on returning my bond. "I ask *in loco parentis.*" He smiled his nasty smile.

I had milked the cows and done the chores in a rush for years so that I could have lessons, but I saw no reason to make haste now. I did not answer him at once.

First, after accepting the canceled document, I ripped it in half and then in half again, and I scattered the scraps like worthless dry leaves in the deacon's great fireplace. He looked scandalized. Could he have thought, perhaps, that I had respect for that loathsome contract? Could he have imagined I would be sentimental about it?

I had been his family's bond slave for ten years, and he was still parroting his *in loco parentis. More locust,* I thought, *like the plague. You have never replaced my father.*

I detested Deacon Thomas.

"I suppose you will choose to marry," he guessed, answering his own question.

"No, I shall not marry, Deacon," I declared with such vehemence his spectacles quivered in surprise. "I shall be an independent spinster." *Answerable only to God, for he is truly my father,* I added in my mind.

Marriage was Mother's idea too, dropped into periodic letters and messages amidst Ben Franklin's wise sayings. Recently she'd written, *"I have come up with a fine suitor for you, the son of a prosperous farmer."*

I shuddered at the thought.

Mistake me not. I believed in love and I dreamed of it. I was prepared to swoon readily if it happened to me.

I had practiced swooning though it seemed a foolish exercise, and one could get bruised.

Yes, I had given the matter of courtship much thought, as young women do. Without love and romance life would be humdrum and dull. True love united souls. That was my vision; one of beauty and blossoms, of closeness in which one looked into the very heart of one's lover.

No, I did not want to marry and be deserted as Mother was. Not now, with freedom just within my grasp.

"I prefer to teach," I spoke out forcefully. "With the men teachers gone to war, if the village elders will have me as teacher, I would live on here and help Mistress Thomas during summer term and teach. The rest of the year I can board with families who need my spinning and weaving and sewing."

I liked the teaching immensely. In addition to sewing and knitting, I edged in some reading and writing for the girls as well as the boys. Together we practiced penmanship. As textbooks I had a Bible, a spelling book, several Psalters, and *The New England Primer*. For pennies I had acquired chapbooks from peddlers, and I read to the students aloud from my own copies of *Gulliver's Travels*, *The Pilgrim's Progress*, and *Robinson Crusoe.*

And I read to them from the newspapers too. One day there was a story about Molly Pitcher, whose name was really Mary Hays. I dramatized it for the students. I transformed myself into Molly with my husband, John, at the battle of Monmouth, New Jersey, and I carried pitchers of water to the soldiers while John fired a cannon. When he collapsed, I resolved, "I, too, can fire this cannon!"

The knitting needle that I used for my pointer became the cannon, and I reloaded and reloaded, remaining there and bravely fighting through the whole battle! The schoolchildren and I all chanted "Ready! Aim! Fire!" together. They were thrilled, so excited, I could not easily quiet them nor could I calm myself. "We cannot say who will be a hero," I told them. "In this case it is a woman."

A large boy objected. "Mistress Sampson, a woman cannot be a hero."

"Yes, you are right," I agreed. "There is another word for Molly Pitcher. She is a *heroine*. Let us learn to say it together and then we will spell it."

So we did. Call her what you will, Molly Pitcher was a hero.

❋ ❋ ❋

I was no longer living with the Thomases. I was staying in the Leonards' house, spinning and weaving their wool for eight pence a day and my keep. I had the Leonards' son Samuel's little back room; he had enlisted. One lucky thing was that my childhood friend, Jennie, was a servant in the Leonards' house. Her owner, Judge Oliver, who'd fled Patriot wrath, had arranged it so that her wages went to him. This was the first time since I'd finished my indenture that I worked alongside Jennie.

She'd gotten so good at reading, I came up with an idea. "When's your birthday, Jennie?" I asked her.

"Don't have one," she said. "Wintertime is all I know. Nobody marked it."

"December seventeenth is my nineteenth birthday. I shall share it with you," I offered. "It's easy to remember; the Boston Tea Party came the day before. The country's birthday and mine and now yours too."

Jennie was delighted.

On December seventeenth, she gave me a lovely cream-colored crocheted scarf she'd made.

From a peddler's saddlebag I'd bought her *The Pilgrim's Progress.* "Happy shared birthday," I said as I handed her the book.

"Oh, Deborah." She held it in her two hands and began to weep over it.

"You're soaking it, girl. It doesn't need a wash."

"It's just—the judge is gone so I can keep it now, but when he comes back to the big house . . ."

I gave her my handkerchief. "Jennie, he's a Tory. He had to run away to England. Maybe he won't ever come back to the big house. Times are changing. Anyway, while you're working here you can keep it, then I'll keep it for you, and you can take it whenever you want it. But it's *your* book."

Her smile was bright as a rainbow. She pressed the volume to her bosom. "Jennie's book! I'm going to write that in it—*big.*"

She did. The letters of her name were bigger than the book's title.

I did something very bold that nineteenth birthday. I took a fearsome step; a giant leap, really. I leaped right out of my church. My examination of my conscience took me from the Congregationalists to the Baptists.

That was a hard bite for Deacon Thomas to swallow. I'd been a faithful Christian. Oh, he'd seen to that. Every Sunday for ten years I'd attended public worship at the

First Congregational Church with the Thomas family, shivering in the winters even though I wore three pairs of drawers for warmth. I trusted the good Lord to forgive my unsacred dress. I listened to the sermons and for long hours I prayed. I observed the Sabbath exactly, without gay or frivolous amusements. I was pious, just a sheep—part of the Congregationalist flock.

But once I was independent and living on my own, I had much free time to consider puzzling questions as I sat all day at the wheel spinning or at the loom weaving: Why was man created? Why was I born? For what purpose? Which way lay my path to salvation?

I longed to be saved. I had private thoughts about God. I saw him and honored him in my own way: not as an arbitrary monarch ruling in the sky, but a power harnessing the whirlwind, blessing the breezes, meting out the lightning and thunder. I believed any clean, quiet place was as good for worship as a church.

I cared not for a one-day religion banished on weekdays and then dressed up all prissy and righteous on the Sabbath.

I believed in Christian principles. But some of Christianity troubled me. The burning of Joan of Arc was always with me. The witch-and-wizard time of

Cotton Mather in nearby Salem disgusted me. That wasn't Christian.

The citizens of Middleborough were forced to pay taxes to the Congregational church, and that seemed unfair to me. Why, we were fighting a war against such taxation! I believed each person should worship where and how he chose.

Further, I was bewildered by the many different Christian sects that all promised: *You will be saved!* First I thought about joining one, then another, and another. I was not able to choose the right one and settle on it. I couldn't tell which was the right one.

All around me, folks were restless and worried and not sure about anything anymore as the war dragged on and on. Searching within oneself—like mine—was common and we were having a great awakening. Meetings commenced at the Third Baptist Church, where I heard Reverend Asa Hunt preach. He thrilled me, conjuring up the vivid glories of God and salvation. My spirit soared on his words. I went back and back again to hear him, daring to hope that I was experiencing grace and my sins were forgiven.

One Sunday morning I got up out of bed, glanced

heavenward, and declared, "Yes, Lord, today I shall become a Baptist." And I did, forthwith.

I couldn't wait. That very night, I walked out to the Thomas farm and made another declaration. "Deacon," I said, "I have come to report, sir, that I have changed my church this day. After much thinking about it, I've become a Baptist."

He stared bewildered at me, as if I were a hen that had dared to crow. "Why did you come all this way to tell me?"

"Because, sir, my father is lost. You are my *in loco parentis*," I said. I was marvelous polite. He could not tell if I was mocking him.

"You *think* too much for a female," he said, then he wet his lips in that mean way of his. "You're a Congregationalist. You've always been one."

"No, sir." I denied it. "I prayed there but I've never committed myself."

"Why—why the Baptists?"

"It feels like the right way for me."

I knew what was coming next, and I was prepared for it.

"What will your mother say?"

"She won't say anything. Her people sailed a long way on the *Mayflower* so that they could choose their own church."

He puckered up his face, but he would comment no more.

I wrote Mother immediately and she did not answer, which meant, of course, that she did not approve. She couldn't quote Ben Franklin at me; he had his own private ideas about freedom in Christianity that were upsetting the Middleborough church people. That was the first time I really liked Ben Franklin.

It was my right to make up my own mind. I knew the Congregationalists were whispering about me, but I didn't care.

Then the dream of the monstrous serpent came to me a second time, in all its dark strangeness. I was again filled with terror. Why me? What did it presage? It had to have meaning. Dreams carry messages, but I could not understand mine. I recognized, however, that it was a warning. Some grave danger was about to befall me. No matter what else it bode, it threatened: Beware, Deborah!

Beware! Beware of what?

Then the immediate danger itself came knocking on the Leonards' door one evening.

A man from Plymouth suddenly appeared: Noah Greene. My mother and his father, with the connivance of Deacon Thomas, must have put him up to it.

He was an ungainly giant of a fellow with colorless tan eyes. He had hair lank as hay and seemed not to own a comb. When he came to call that first late afternoon, there was liquor already on his breath, and during the evening, which we spent at the village inn, he drank a great deal more. *Ah, Mother,* I thought bitterly, *I am a give-away child, but would you give me to him?* His tongue was thick and dull in speech. I did not care for him from first glance. I thought him a lump of a man. A dolt. So *he* was all Mother thought I was worth.

Alas, he seemed taken with me. He insisted on standing back-to-back against me so that he could take my measure. "You are uncommon tall," he marveled. "We were measured out by the Almighty."

"It's an accident. Tallness runs in families," I observed, but he didn't take notice of my scoffing.

"An accident made in heaven," he said and then belched, laughing at his own body's accomplishment.

I was contrary and sullen, and I drank three tumblers of rum, which I'd never done before, at his cost, as I did my best to discourage him.

When he went off, I watched him go with joy. I had been as disagreeable as possible. Surely he would not want me. I had no dowry or land or family wealth. Could *he* be what the dread dream was warning of? If so, had my rude behavior discouraged him? Oh, how I hoped so.

I had ample free time to wander about by myself when I wasn't working. But a young woman dared not walk out on the roads to explore and have adventures after dusk or in the early morning.

I soon devised a brave means of doing so. Sam Leonard's clothes lay in an unlocked trunk aside the bed. He was tall and slim, just about equal to my size. The clothes kept tempting me, saying, "Come on, Deborah, try us on. Nobody's using us anyway." Every time I came in or went out, there were those clothes looking me in the face. One night I slipped on his shirt just as a lark. Perfect. Next, I tried on his hat. My hair was hard to put up neatly but the hat fit exactly, as if made for my head.

Next came the breeches. I made sure my door was locked and put a chair up against it as well. I slipped my feet into them very slowly and then pulled them up to my waist, fearing the clap of thunder, the bolt of lightning of the Almighty. I'd done some bold things in my life, but I'd never assailed the decency of my Puritan ancestors. I knew they'd think it sinful and Mother would surely think so, as well as Deacon Thomas and my own minister, Reverend Asa Hunt, and all the parishioners.

I sat on Sam's bed then, my eyes shut, awaiting retribution. When nothing happened, I slid the boots right onto my feet.

Kneeling and bending and kicking my feet high like a loosed stallion, I stepped around and danced and whirled and jumped, rejoicing in the deliverance of the breeches. I felt strong. No man was more beautiful in his breeches than I. In the mirror I could see that I was graceful. During the ten years I'd lived with the Thomases and laundered hundreds of pairs of breeches, I had dreamed of trying on a pair, but I would not dare do it in the deacon's house.

Sam's pants had set me free!

When I got buttoned into his suit, I found it a close fit but comfortable. I couldn't bring myself to undress, to take off those wonderful clothes, so I slept all night in Sam's suit.

In the morning I made up my mind to borrow the clothes. First, I had to design and sew an undergarment compressing my chest. I have small breasts so it was not too difficult a task. I fashioned a tight linen cloth, shoulder to waist, buckled in the back. If I donned this male garb, then once night began to fall I could set out for nearby towns and villages and walk upon the roads safely. I trembled with anticipation at the prospect, but I held myself back and did not act immediately.

It was necessary for me to study the behavior of the men all around me, so I could imitate it. I practiced in front of the mirror. I had to learn everything anew: walking, sitting, bending, drinking, even the way I used my arms and hands, and, of course, talking.

Talking was especially hard. My voice was ordinarily not high, but I had to learn to speak from deep in my throat. I could not yell; that sound was shrill, a sure giveaway, and I could never allow myself to giggle. Never!

I drilled myself as I recited aloud, watching my reflection and listening to myself hour after hour.

Then, in my manly costume, feeling like the boldest girl in the colonies, I occasionally began to slip away at twilight and explore places—close by at first, then a bit farther. I was always careful to watch the time; Mr. Leonard was set in his ways and went to bed early. He locked the front door exactly at the stroke of ten.

Entering a tavern, I would sit in the shadows drinking

a small glass of beer and listening to returned soldiers talking. Sometimes I ordered rum, a drink for both men and women, and I could stay a long time over my single drink. Nowhere was I noticed or recognized.

One very early morn I'd walked to Taunton and was making my way back when I saw on the road ahead of me, advancing straight toward me, a Middleborough citizen, William Bennett. I would have hidden but he'd already seen me approaching. There was nothing to be done but to greet him bold-faced and walk on. Quaking with fear, I hurriedly plucked some ragweed and inhaled. As I came near to him, I was seized with the beginning of a great sneeze, so I buried my face in my sleeve. "God bless," he called out, and I murmured, "Thank you, sir," and went my way, hastening my steps. He did not know me. God, indeed, had already blessed me with that sneeze. I returned home joyful. Oh, how much I wanted to tell someone, but I could not.

The very next day I began to weave cloth of brown fustian to make my own suit of clothes. I wove industriously and soon started the tailoring. Mistress Thomas had taught me to sew with skill and this was a sewing job I relished. I had no plan at the time. I just wanted a disguise.

Soon after, I took a second daring step.

The need to tell someone burned fiercely inside me. I decided to confide in Jennie.

"Jennie," I said one afternoon, "I've a secret to tell you."

"Good." She grinned. "I miss your secrets. You may be grown now but you ain't changed."

I whispered, "I have Sam Leonard's suit hid in my room in a trunk. And sometimes I wear it and go about in it in the early mornings or evenings."

"Like a ha'nt to scare folks?"

"No. Like a man."

"You ain't changed." Jennie looked really awed.

"And I just wove some cloth for myself, so I could make my own suit."

"Suit? With britches?"

I nodded.

"If they catch you out—you know what folks think 'bout women wearin' britches. Ain't nothin' worse."

"I don't care what they think. But they won't catch me. The other morning on the road from Taunton, Mr. William Bennett came upon me walking in Sam's suit."

Jennie looked horrified. "Oh, Lord. What did you do? What did you say?"

"I just quick breathed in some ragweed and sneezed something fierce into my sleeve. He blessed me and I went on my way. He never knew me."

"He blessed you?" Jennie couldn't help but laugh. "Why you doin' this, Deb?" she wondered. "It's so dangerous."

"I don't really know. But all day while I'm spinning, my head spins dreams of faraway cities like Boston and New York. I think about how grand it would be to see the new capital of the United States, Philadelphia! And the other wonderful places I've already visited in my head."

"You're like a wild bird," she said quietly. "You got to flap your wings else you die. I know the feelin' but a blackbird's wings are cut. I bless you too, Deborah, for flyin' for us all."

"I might not fly far, Jennie, but you're right, I've got to try. Listen—I hear there's a fortune-teller set up in the inn at Four Corners. I mean to put on Sam's clothes tonight and have my fortune told."

"Why?"

"Because a fortune-teller can see everything. If I fool this fortune-teller, if he can't see through me, then I'll know my masquerade works. I need help with dressing, especially with tying up my hair. Are you brave enough to help me get ready?"

"No. But a coward could tie up your hair—and I will."

And Jennie was as good as her word.

That night, after supper, the Leonards went to church. Jennie came to my room, where I had Sam's clothes laid out on the patchwork quilt.

Once I was in them, Jennie was amazed. "You're a fine-looking fellow," she said. "Girls are going to take to you like flies to molasses," she teased. "Then what'll you do?"

"Nothing. They'll get stuck," I said, and we both laughed. "Come on, Jennie. Will you do up my hair in a queue?"

She went right to it and did a fine tight job. I put on the hat and I almost didn't know my own self. "Will the fortune-teller be able to see through me?" I wondered.

"I think you're goin' to do all right, Deb. I feel it. But how will you get back in if you're late? After Mr. Leonard locks up?"

"You're in the room above the porch, Jennie. If you leave your window open—and if you don't mind—I can climb up from the porch if I'm locked out. I'll be very quiet and try not to wake you."

"You better wake me if I'm sleeping, which I won't be with you out there with a fortune-teller. Good luck," she whispered as I slipped out. "This is a mighty big flap, Deb. You're almost flyin'."

In the warm darkness of the spring night, I walked the half mile to the inn without difficulty, and, once inside, I looked around in the smoky light till I saw a tall, skinny fellow with raggedy black hair sitting alone at a table aside the fireplace. He had some charts spread out before him. There was a wild look to him, sitting there in the firelight in his big oxhide shirt with rips and bullet holes in it. He looked part Indian. A broad, jagged scar cut his right eyebrow in two bristly halves and traveled up to his scalp. The knife must have just missed his eye.

He was a scamp. In skirts, Deborah Sampson would not ever have talked to or gone near him.

I hitched up my breeches and swaggered the best I knew how as I moved closer. "I hear you tell fortunes?" I started.

"That I do."

"How much?"

"Five pence."

I dug out the coins and set them down.

"Sit," he said, "and give me your birth date."

"December seventeenth."

He studied his charts, which had all sorts of queer lines and circles and arrows on them. "You are born under Sagittarius, the archer," he said. "You're a restless man with a longin' to travel." Here he stopped to fill and light his pipe and then he smoked for a bit, gazing at the fire.

Was he through with me? For five pence, I thought, I deserved to hear a bit more. Yet I feared delay, for any minute I might be found out.

"What do you do?" he asked me suddenly. "You don't seem a farmer."

Maybe he *could* see what other men didn't.

"I teach school," I said. "My father was a farmer, but I've bigger dreams." I led him away from the farm. "Will I get to do the traveling?" I asked.

"Let me look at your hand."

I hadn't expected that. He might find it a feminine hand, though it was calloused and rough enough from hard work. Hesitantly, I opened my palm and he studied it.

"Yes, you will travel," he said, "and you will also have to fight bravely. You will encounter many hard times."

"That is the fortune of all of mankind," I said, withdrawing my hand and rising from my chair.

He stared at me hard but did not reproach me for my challenge. "Some suffer more than others. You are one of those. Persist," he said. "I see you are a stubborn fellow."

I took my leave of him and hastened home.

The door was already bolted fast. With Sam's boots strung about my neck, I climbed noiselessly from the porch roof into Jennie's room. True to her word she was awake, kneeling in the darkness waiting for me.

"I've been repeatin' the Psalm we learned together," she whispered. "'The Lord is my shepherd, I shall not want.' Deb, could he tell?" she asked.

"No. The clothes worked beautifully. He told me a young man's fortune."

Jennie smothered her laugh in a pillow. "What was the fortune?"

"That I'll travel and have adventures and many troubles."

"Oh, I'm so sorry."

"Jennie, don't worry. He can't be such a good fortune-teller, can he, if I fooled him?"

"Still, it's scary to get a bad fortune."

"Thanks for helping," I said. "No one ever had a better friend."

She clasped me to her. "That's the nicest thing I've ever been, your friend. I'll help you when the real troubles come."

Neither of us had any idea that I'd need her help so soon.

Noah Greene returned to see me again. "You are as tall as I am," he observed wittily.

"True," I said. "I didn't shrink a bit these past weeks though it rained considerable."

He grunted and pondered as he tried to catch hold of my meaning. *You wouldn't know a jest if it attacked you directly,* I thought in disgust. He was content to sit beside me on the bench at the trestle table, head lowered like a cow at a trough, drinking silently.

I sipped my hard cider and tried to think of a way to make the time pass. "What do you like to read?" I inquired of him.

"Read?" He laughed. "Grown men have no time for

readin'. Schoolboys read." He chortled at my stupidity, and then he perfectly aimed a great stream of tobacco juice into the spittoon. He was showing me that was what grown men did.

I tried next to speak of the war, truly a subject for grown men, but he cared naught about the war. He seemed to care naught about anything except the drink and, unfortunately, *tall* me. My height absolutely captivated him. Here was this foul-breathed stranger suddenly mumbling about "our happy future" and "all the lovely, tall, fair babies" we'd have together. The man was somehow unhinged.

Several weeks later, he appeared a third time. He was sober and had a grim face. He confided that he'd just come from a talk with Deacon Thomas. I was alarmed. First, why had he seen Deacon Thomas? Then he uttered these ominous words.

"This time I bear heavy news from your mother."

"Oh, is Mother ill? Has she lost her place? Has something happened to one of the babies?"

"Hold, hold, girl," he said, looking a little foolish.

"What *heavy* news?" I demanded.

"It is that she lacks—that she lacks—"

"What does she lack?"

"Grandchildren!" His face cracked into a grin. "Your mother lacks grandchildren." He guffawed, slapping his thigh with glee.

Mr. Blockhead had actually made a joke!

If this Noah had an ark, I'd bore a hole in it. If Mother loved me, how dared she match me with such a dullard? Marriage to him would be worse than indenture. It would be out-and-out slavery!

I could not bear him another minute. I had to cut this visit short. "I feel faint," I said, pressing my brow with my hand. "I must go in and rest."

"But I came this long way. . . ."

Who asked you to? I thought, but I kept still. Then I suggested brightly, "Perhaps you can stop off at the inn for refreshment." That cheered him.

Walking beside me, concealed by the dense brush, Noah grabbed me suddenly and attempted to kiss me, slavering all over my cheek. It felt like lukewarm, slimy soup. I pulled away violently.

"What's wrong with you, girl? We're promised—" he muttered.

"I'm promised to no one but myself," I rejoined, and I hastened inside to scrub my face with soap and water. There was no question about the danger I was in. Every free minute I had after that mauling, I worked at finishing my suit and gathering the rest of my disguise. I would have to flee. And do it immediately.

Alas, my unwelcome suitor and the prospect of marrying him had so unsettled and upset me, I couldn't think clearly. I was furious, burning with indignation and fear.

He had *not* asked me so I had *not* turned him down, but I recognized that I would have to get away. He was well named Noah. He had NOah mind, NOah beauty, NOah wit. And he was a drunkard.

My despair over Noah was surely the cause of the return of the serpent dream—a third time so soon after the second. I trembled and my body grew cold when the unearthly voice once again bade me to gird myself.

The first dream had come to me when I was very young, and it had terrified me.

The second had troubled me greatly, for I was older and sensed something big was being asked of me, but I could not fathom what.

But thrice?

The number three, everyone knows, is magical and signals that the message comes straight from God! This dream was an omen, a sacred portent.

So when I heard the recruiter's music sounding on the Middleborough green the very next evening at sunset, and I looked out my window and saw a young soldier fling his saddlebag atop his horse and mount and fly off, I donned Sam's clothing for the final time, tied up my hair, and set forth. I didn't seek out Jennie to tell her, for I feared she would try to stop me.

To add to my deep despair, a great black tomcat suddenly leaped right across my path as I stepped onto the grass. He crouched and snarled, his green eyes glaring at me; then he tore off into the brush. Immediately, I spat thrice quickly over my left shoulder. The evil power of black cats is awesome. Spitting forcefully lessens the danger, wise old women advise. There is no other known remedy.

Were it not for the dream—and Noah—that cat crossing my path would have turned me right around and made me abandon my plans. But I was trapped.

I could not go back. I forced my leaden feet to move forward to the Woodses' house, where the recruiter had set up shop on the porch.

I had no trouble at first, for the recruiter, who was not a local man, welcomed me. I told him I was sixteen and longed to enlist.

"Your name?" he inquired.

"Timothy Thayer." I'd made it up beforehand. I liked the sound.

"Come sign the paper and you'll get your bounty money."

I took the pen and began to sign.

"How odd it is," remarked old Mistress Woods, rocking in her chair across from the desk, "this Timothy Thayer holds his pen queer with the middle finger stiff, the same way Deborah Sampson, my grandchildren's teacher, held her pen."

Oh, hush, old woman, I prayed inwardly. *Oh, hush!* Her words made me feel all hollow inside. The black cat had worked its demonic evil.

The busy recruiter did not heed her mumbling. He was counting out the bounty money to pay me. "Muster in two weeks," he said, and I took my departure.

Immediately, second thoughts engulfed me. I wished to undo that enlistment! I had been hasty and stupid and now I was in deep trouble. How could I serve with local Middleborough youths? They—surely more quickly than any others—would see through my mummery. But I had the bounty money in my pocket. In two weeks Timothy Thayer would have to serve.

✻   ✻   ✻

The nights and days of the next fortnight were frightful, my mind flip-flopping. First, I'd think to chance it and go, then next minute I'd decide against. And then I would and then I wouldn't. I could not determine what to do.

Mother sent a note that Noah was coming courting once more and I had best behave properly. Jennie helped me dot my face and arms with a pink birthwort salve so that I looked terrible. I came forth and Noah hastened to kiss my cheek, as I had anticipated. He got a taste of the foulest of herbs.

"I have this dreadful rash all over me," I complained, "and a high fever as well, but it is naught. I was so eager to see you."

He drew back. "Could it be pox?" Too late he scrubbed his mouth with the back of his hand.

"It could," I conceded.

"I was just passing by," he said hastily. "I stopped in for a minute, but I am needed elsewhere."

"Let me know if you catch it," I said. "Look out for spots. One never knows. . . ." He did not try to kiss me good-bye. I pouted and he fled.

*   *   *

The omens and portents of the dream were unmistakable, yet when muster time came and I heard the music calling us to arms, I could not bring myself to report. I stayed locked in my room. After several hours, I heard a fierce knocking.

"Deborah, it's me. Jennie. I've been on the green. They're looking for Timothy Thayer, who took bounty money and has not appeared for muster."

"Why should that concern a spinster like me?"

"Because"—she whispered—"old Mistress Woods has been saying all over town that Timothy Thayer held a pen odd just like you."

I unbolted the door.

Jennie's eyes were bright with fear. "She told your minister, Reverend Hunt, and he was so angry he said, 'If what you say is true and Deborah Sampson wears breeches, then we Baptists will cast her out of our flock.'

"They'll be looking for you next, Deb. They are all mighty angry about your wearin' britches. And Mistress Woods is tellin' that they're Sam's britches you stole."

"I didn't steal. I borrowed."

"The Leonards say they'll burn the clothes if you wore them. There's much anger about."

"Oh, Jennie, you must help me. Take the bounty money back to the recruiter. Tell him only that a strange lad stopped you in the road and asked you to return it from Timothy Thayer, who cannot serve." I thrust the money at her. "Please, go at once," I begged.

"And what will you do, Deb?"

"I will fly," I said. "Good-bye, dear friend. Go quickly for my sake. And do not tell them my secret."

"They know," she said sadly. "They already know."

Hurriedly, I took my Bible from beneath my pillow. "This is for you, Jennie. A keepsake. You must find a hiding place for it and your *Pilgrim's Progress*."

She clutched it to her. "I will say our Twenty-third Psalm for you every night. I will never tell. Never," she promised tearfully. "I swear. Never, even if they whip me."

"You have been my best friend all my life, Jennie," I said, and we clung together for an instant, before she ran off to the green to save me from the recruiter and the villagers and my angry minister.

In a frenzy, I bound my bosom and tied up my hair, then dressed in my own suit of brown fustian, and, taking my savings, I sneaked out to hide in the deep brush until darkness descended and I could chance walking upon the roads.

I, Deborah Sampson—give-away child, bond servant, unwilling choice of Noah Greene, betrayed by my own signature—had to run from here forever.

4. *Fortune's Fool*

Into the black night I went, the moon and stars concealed by swollen, gray summer clouds. I was grateful for the shadows. I headed furtively along the stagecoach road southeast toward New Bedford, thinking wildly that I might survive by getting work on a sailing ship. This hope was a mark of my desperation, for I greatly feared the storms at sea that roiled my dreams. Yet, I had to escape—and fast. I was fortune's fool.

When daylight came, I crawled into a thicket, supplied with a meager bun from a stagecoach inn. Trudging along those rutted roads in the heavy work boots of my *in loco parentis* days had wearied my legs fearfully. Oh, how I wished I had softer walking boots! But I slept, and when I woke I was restored. I proceeded again under cover of darkness until at long last I was in New Bedford.

The sea air sharp with salt was exhilarating and reminded me of my father, lured away by distance and adventure. Before me was a vast harbor with shipyards surrounding it. Who knew but I might yet meet Father or one who had word of him, in just such an unlikely place as this. My excitement overcame my weariness and nighttime fears. Locked inland on the farm, I had only read of such vast places.

Again, hunger took me to an inn, and, careful of my pence, I bought biscuits and broth. Already breakfasting near where I sat was a single man, a scowling, skeletal giant clad in a blue coat with brass buttons and wearing a peaked cap.

Appreciating the rest, I ate my meager meal slowly, inhaling the aromas of his bacon and eggs, flapjacks and molasses. I did not dare to interrupt him till he had finished all but his drink. Then, I approached. "Pardon, sir. Do you know of a ship in the harbor that needs a hand?"

He stared at me balefully. "I am captain of such a ship bound for Jamaica."

"I am seeking work," I said.

"Can you cook?"

I nodded. "I had no mother to cook for me."

He drummed on the table with his fingers.

"Jim, my first mate, is waiting on the dock with the stores," he said. "You go down there and sit with him. I'll be along and we'll sign you up."

Down I went speedily and came upon a gray-bearded fellow looking out to sea. "Are you Jim?" I asked.

"Who wants to know?"

"Timothy Thayer."

"Timothy, eh? I had a younger brother, Timothy. Sweet boy. Died of the pox before he was three."

"Sorry," I said.

"So, Timothy—what do you want with me?"

"The captain told me to wait here with you. He's hired me as second cook on this voyage."

His face brightened. "That's good 'cause the first cook is a drunk who burns water wonderful well." He smiled at his own sally. "What dishes can you cook best?"

"I make a good Irish stew and chicken soup with potato dumplings."

"Potato dumplings, eh?" He smacked his lips at that, glad that I was coming aboard. But then, as we talked further and he found out I'd never worked on a ship or traveled anywhere before, he grew quieter and became more serious.

"Timothy, me boy, you better think twice about signin' on. The captain is a drinkin' man and he's a brute with his fists when he's drunk. The ship is a hell and he's the devil himself! I've been sailing with him for twenty years and I know. You talk more like a gentleman's son than a sailor. It's not the place for a lad like you. You'd best flee while you can—"

"But why don't you flee?" I asked boldly. "You've had twenty years of it, you say."

"Some men have nowhere to run." He opened his gnarled hands flat before him. "I'm giving you the same advice I'd give my own sweet brother. Go now before it's too late."

I saw such deep misery in the first mate's eyes and in the sunken set of his mouth that, without further ado, I rose and moved away hastily.

Looking back at the lone figure sitting on the stone jetty, I saw him raise his hand high and wave me forward, away. Increasing my speed, I was soon a safe distance. My feelings were all a jumble—sadness for this stranger who'd cared about me, but happiness that I'd carried it off.

I'd fooled them all.

My disguise had deceived various canny men: my neighbor William Bennett, the fortune-teller, the recruiter in Middleborough, the tavern keepers who sold me food and drink, and now these two hardened seamen. I took heart that I would be able to enlist and serve.

Boldly, I resolved to walk all the way to Boston, which I so longed to see, and enlist there. I had studied maps and knew it was about fifty miles as the crow flies, but this crow was walking and often on very roundabout roads. My decision meant a complete shift in direction. I'd have to walk north some seventy miles. My savings were pretty much gone but I was encouraged by the knowledge that there would be work along the way, for many young men were off the land at war. The one good thing I knew absolutely was that I could work as hard as any lad. Harder.

So I walked along, hiring myself out to tend cows and horses and labor in fields or in vegetable gardens. I helped haul rocks away to clear the fields and I built a boundary fence of those same rocks. I chopped several cords of firewood.

"Stay on and work," folks urged me often. "Timothy Thayer, there is a place for you here. Welcome."

I politely refused, mindful of my private goal: Boston within three weeks' time. "Timothy Thayer" could not afford to linger, to answer questions, or to make friends. Though I had to walk wearily all through the last night, I kept to my calendar.

I caught my breath at first sight of the grand church spires as Boston stood before me, the great city with its more than fifteen thousand citizens. My feet clopped along the middle post road, my dusty boots unused to cobblestones.

I had to see *everything*.

Bostonians, proud of their city, were pleased to point out the customs house, Faneuil Hall, and King's Chapel. I had not imagined anything as marvelous as this city. There I stood, my nose pressed against the window of Paul Revere's shop, admiring the silver. I strolled on Beacon Street among elegant ladies and gentlemen. Even perhaps alongside John Hancock, who, a citizen said, dwelled there. John Hancock, first signer of the Declaration of Independence! Like Jennie, John Hancock wrote mighty big. His letters made his name so large King George might be able to read it without glasses. How clever that was!

The city with its splendid homes and shops and people, many of whom I did not understand, for they spoke strange tongues, thrilled me. Several times I ran across folks indentured as I had been—laboring and waiting for their freedom. They'd bartered the years of their lives for passage across the ocean.

Whatever hardships would come upon me henceforth, seeing Boston made them worthwhile.

"Which way to the Old North Church?" I asked a newsboy one evening. He couldn't have been more than seven years old.

He pointed the way, then grinned at me and shouted, "One if by land and two if by sea," and galloped off as if on horseback.

With my money dwindling, I could not stay longer, but the desire to explore more of Massachusetts kept me still on the road, and I wandered through Roxbury and Dedham. In Bellingham, bordering Rhode Island, I decided to cast my last few pence on a breakfast of corn muffins and molasses and a cup of chicory, after which I was determined to enlist.

While I rested and sipped my hot drink, a tall, well-dressed stranger kept staring at me. Did he know me? Had I been found out? How could I escape? My cup was empty but I still tipped it up and pretended to swallow. Finally, he accosted me. "Are you a veteran?"

"No, not I," I responded. "Though I am thinking of signing up."

"Well, this is a lucky meeting then, for I am helping the recruiter make up the quota for Uxbridge."

I knew at once he was a speculator. Each community had to send so many men, and speculators worked on commission going about seeking recruits. He was a man who had to know much about the army. I listened closely to him.

"Enlisting is a good move for you. You get to travel about to all different places, and you get food and board, and a uniform free. Besides that there is a large bounty. Sixty pounds!"

Not really. He would get a portion of that as his fee, I knew. He was earning it as he talked.

"I've a horse and cart. Let me drive you the few miles to where they're recruiting," he offered.

"Is there a physical examination?" I asked.

"No. They just look you over to see if you pass muster," he replied. "They don't look close. Everybody passes muster. They need volunteers."

I followed him out and off we went.

The recruiting officer welcomed me. General Washington had issued a call for twenty thousand volunteers and few had responded; this officer needed me.

"Name?" he asked.

"Robert Shurtliff" came to my lips. Thus did I hope to do honor to my lost elder brother and please my mother as well. Except that somehow I never managed to please her, and, even as I spoke, I feared she would hate my doing this.

"Have you ever fired a musket?"

"I've hunted deer, wild turkey, and rabbit," I answered honestly, with pride.

I was more than twenty years old but I had to lie and swear that I was only just past seventeen, to explain the fact that my cheeks were still innocent of the scrape of a razor. My fair hair, sky blue eyes, and pale complexion belied my real age. The lie was helped because I now stood very tall and was strong, slim-hipped, and agile. Deacon Thomas, in exacting so much work from me, had assisted the transformation from dependent and helpless maiden to eligible recruit.

How he would have hated to know that! If only there were a way to tell him.

"You get sixty pounds bounty money," the officer said, cheerfully counting it out for me but withholding the speculator's fee.

The speculator took his pittance, which he had

surely earned, and then set out immediately to hunt for more recruits.

The officer handed me a long paper entitled *Articles of Enlistment*. "Note it is an enlistment for three years," he advised.

I nodded.

Some occasions are blessed. This was one such.

No fierce black tomcat this night leaped out to hex me, nor was there any troublesome old busybody woman to notice the way I held a pen when I signed my name.

"Robert Shurtliff, you are now a member of the Fourth Massachusetts Regiment of the Continental army. As soon as we have our complement, we march to train in New York. Our base will be West Point."

I felt very proud. "I am ready, sir."

Then, feeling a great sadness, I wandered aside where none could see me, and with my hunting knife, I hacked off my hair. *It is for your country, Deborah,* I comforted myself to stop my weeping.

There were fifty of us volunteers on that twelve-day march over rough country with little rest. We were a mixed group, youths and mature men, many of them veterans. We shared a fellowship such as I had never known, all of us struggling along together on muddy rutted roads: weary, dirty, hungry, lacking proper sleep, all determined to save our newborn country.

And singing often as we moved ahead, the very song that the British troops in their fancy red coats had brought with them from England, making fun of us as rustics.

> *Yankee Doodle went to town*
> *A-riding on a pony;*
> *He stuck a feather in his hat*
> *And called it macaroni.*

In King George's court, the fops and dandies over-dressed in Italian finery called macaroni. So we stole their song, keeping their mocking words and turning them into our own proud anthem. Many of us stuck feathers in our ragged caps. Mine was a handsome blue jay feather. I loved my macaroni.

We passed burned farmhouses and barns pillaged by Tories. Plodding along the road with us were victims, families made wanderers by war, as well as tattered women and children, camp followers—a sorry lot.

Friendships sprung up quickly among the men. I

tried to be polite and helpful yet keep my distance. The older men had their joke on me sometimes, calling me "Bloomin' Boy" or "Smock-faced Boy" because I was so fair-skinned and blond.

One day I got hold of a precious copy of *The Boston Gazette* and was reading the news when several of the others clamored, "Read us about the war." Few of the recruits had been schooled, so I read aloud and after that they respected me more. I became a public reader and even wrote letters for some who could not write. I could sew a button on, too, and I did for some, but I didn't want to be noticed for womanish tasks. I had to be manly.

Another young volunteer, Roger Snow, out of Concord, a tall, quiet lad with loneliness in his eyes, sought me out and befriended me. "You read with great ease and fire," he said. "I, too, am bookish. Father thought it was a fault in a farmer."

He had curly hair black as coal and thickly lashed dark eyes to match. Roger had an endearing intensity about him. He cared passionately about ideas, about freedom and justice and about reasons for the way people behaved. Most of the other recruits were more like my suitor, Noah Greene. They did not bother to think at all. I liked Roger at once, the more because he told me he'd had no women in his life, his mother dying at his birth.

I had to keep my distance. Fortunately, he was himself a private fellow, so he respected my privacy. He had sensitivity, thoughtfulness, and intelligence, all that Noah, the oaf Mother had chosen for me, lacked.

From first glance, my woman's heart began to plague me: *Ah, if instead of numbskull Noah. . . .* I silently mourned what might have been.

Military life had its constant routines. We exercised and drilled intensely. During our training, for leisure sport, someone introduced arm wrestling and it became the most popular pastime among my comrades. Of course, I refused all challenges that meant body contact, and there was great teasing. To my amazement, Roger would not wrestle either and there were fresh catcalls and more teasing.

"I'm saving my arms to wrestle Tories," Roger argued.

"What kind of Tories?" some fellow jibed.

"All sizes and all shapes," Roger rejoined. "Better than you can possibly imagine."

There was some hooting, but they let him be.

Afterward, I told him quietly, "You did not have to give up arm wrestling for me."

He looked surprised. "I did not do it for you. I hate brutality."

"But you're a volunteer."

"Yes. It's my country I love, not war. My hope is that I can serve it by being a scout instead of a killer."

He pursued our friendship though I did my best to keep it in check.

All I had ever longed for was right here next to me in this dear fellow, whom I had to deceive from the very first minute. Though I tried to maintain distance, we became fast friends, sharing rations and tasks and talking, ever talking. He had a restless mind like my own. I had to be doubly cautious with him, all the while I felt blessed by his company. I was treading lightly but dangerously, indeed, tiptoeing on cracked eggs.

Almost immediately I began to consider: *Surely I must tell him, but how? He will turn from me with revulsion. I could not bear that. I must tell him, but not just yet. I must tell him soon. I must tell him tomorrow.*

Each tomorrow became the next tomorrow. I postponed the truth to enjoy the sweetness of the friendship, and weeks flew by.

One windy night, I had a small misadventure. We'd stopped our long march to rest at a tavern, and I was so fatigued, I suddenly dropped to the floor in a faint. "Help me carry this poor fellow," the young wife of the tavern keeper cried out, cradling my head in her lap. "He requires a good bed. He shall sleep in my place alongside my husband, who is already asleep. I will bed down with my child."

I heard her words but did not protest, for I felt Roger lifting me and my pulse quickened. It was a sweet passage. He placed my arms around his neck. I feigned unconsciousness so that he had to hold me close and carry me aloft to lay me down beside the large, snoring host.

"You must sleep next to a trumpeting elephant, Bobby," he whispered as he set me down softly, removing my hat and brushing my hair from my brow.

Who would not sleep sound after such a tucking-in? The innkeeper snored away unawares. Ah, if Mother— or the deacon—could have seen me, an innocent maiden sharing this bed!

At dawn we went our weary way.

In New York, they were lining us up to receive our uniforms from the quartermaster general. It was a terribly slow process. "You get on line," I told Roger, explaining that I had a sudden cramp.

"I will hold you a place," he offered.

"No, don't. You go ahead, for I cannot say how long I will be." I went off into the woods and had a quick private bath in a secluded pond. I delayed long enough to turn up at the end of the line, so I was nowhere near Roger during his dressing and undressing. I received my regimental coat of linen, dark blue, the indigo complementing my eyes. It was a color I'd always favored. There was a white trim on the coat's lapels and a white lining. My waistcoat and breeches were of white linen. The breeches would fit tight to my legs and cover my ankles.

I rejoiced, remembering my earlier adventures in Sam Leonard's suit. I recognized the value of the gift I was given.

Women who have worn only skirts could never imagine the great freedom and comfort that these breeches allow. I could have climbed a ladder or squatted in the middle of the road, the most indecent way for a girl to sit, and I'd be perfectly modest in pants.

Suddenly no posture or movement, no step or climb or jump, would be immodest. Was it possible that men, knowing full well the beauty and comfort of their breeches, had selfishly kept them from us? They might keep all our petticoats and corsets and garters in exchange, for all I cared.

Square-toed black leather boots with buckles, along with white wool stockings, completed the outfit, except, last and best, for the glorious light infantry hat. It had a black plume tipped in red on one side, and a variegated black and white union cockade on the other.

Of course I tried on the hat at once in front of a glass. It was safe now with my cropped hair. I had to hide my pleasure at the hat's beauty. It was more becoming than any bonnet. If I'd still had my long hair and it was unbraided and brushed loose, it would have been captivating. Still, I looked dauntless but pretty. After smiling several different, engaging smiles at the charming image, I quickly removed the hat and tried not to think such vain, futile thoughts. The function of this hat was to make me look brave, not pretty.

Then it was my time to change into the uniform. I was uneasy. I glanced about—Roger was nowhere in sight. All around me the last of the men were now taking off their clothes. I then kept my eyes fixed to the ground, not that it would have been new or shocking for me to see a man's body. I had bathed and diapered young boys thousands of times. I had been awake through many summer nights when the impetuous Thomas youths, with neither the time nor inclination to stop for breeches, had run naked through the attic to the outhouse. I knew what a nude man's body looked like and was not afraid of it.

I cast my eyes down in true discomfort, fearing not so much that I would look on nude men as that *I* would be seen and *my* disguise destroyed. Fortunately, the new uniforms intrigued the men; no one noticed me. They were all busy admiring themselves and I managed myself skillfully.

Neither undergarments nor sleeping clothes were issued to us. What a relief! It meant we would not have to change garments. We were to live, six men to a tent, in these same clothes day and night.

The long march and heavy exercising had taken their toll on me; no sooner had we settled in the tent than I was afflicted with my monthly period. I suffered terrible cramps and sudden heavy blood loss.

At the drumroll that called reveille, I told Roger, "I cannot go to roll call. I'm not well. It's that faintness I felt in the inn come back again. I just need to rest. I'll be fine in a few hours. Tell the sergeant."

Roger brought me fresh drinking water, then hurried

off with the others while I retrieved one of the small cloths I had hidden in my pack and made myself safe and comfortable. I lay there alone all morning.

At noon, on returning from drill, Roger was mirthful. "Bobby, I've a story for you that will surely cheer you. When I got to the drill ground, there was a great hulking fellow standing about up front searching faces as if he had lost his best friend. I was headed for the sergeant to explain your absence and got to him just as he began interrogating this stranger: 'What business have you here?' he demanded.

" 'I am looking for my runaway bride,' the ruffian said."

Fear clutched my heart as Roger interrupted his tale with laughter. Of course, I said nothing.

" 'You are seeking her in a strange place. We have only men here. Recruits,' the sergeant informed him.

" 'She might be clad as a man. Her name is Deborah Sampson, but she uses the false name also of Timothy Thayer. She is promised to me,' the fellow said.

" 'If she were my betrothed, I would not seek her,' the sergeant advised him, much entertained. 'I would shun her. I would not wed a woman wearing britches.'

"The stranger scratched his head. 'Aye,' he said, 'but she is marvelous tall.'

"'Well, your Deborah/Timothy is not here, so you must go,' said the sergeant, and then he ordered me to leave along with the fellow to see him out of the camp.

"'I would beat her for the britches,' the fellow vowed to me as we parted. 'I would—but she is uncommon tall.'"

Laughing, Roger shook his head at the idiocy of it, and, nervously, I joined in his laughter. Fate had played me many strange tricks, but this was surely the strangest.

I rose as soon as I could and went about my business making light of my morning's pains. I wondered if my mother had sent Noah to seek me. I hoped so. I had thought about writing her many times, but I could not tell her my situation. Perhaps it would be best, I decided, to relieve her mind with a letter assuring her I was well and in good hands. And so, that evening, I wrote the following:

June 16, 1782

Dear Mother,

I am sorry I did not make my farewells to you and the babies, and I also regret my hasty departure, which I could not help.

I have employment in a large, respectable household. My chores are very different from what they were at the Thomas farm, but I do not find them disagreeable. My employers are strict disciplinarians, and I have learned new skills but have many more to learn.

I have done well because I learned from my elders' excellent example. You need not worry about me. I follow the virtuous and prudent models Ben Franklin offered.

I pray for peace and true independence for our country.

Your obedient daughter,
Deborah

I gave the letter to a traveler headed to New York City and had his promise he would mail it there.

The following months were the happiest of my life. I had a true friend living right beside me, the two of us engaged in a noble cause. In order to survive this close living, I had to scheme and plan, and, with nature's cooperation, I went undetected, just another recruit in training.

After that hairbreadth escape from Noah, my monthly bleeding slackened and then became irregular, and after a time it did not occur at all; it was as if my body recognized I was living a rough male life and accommodated to it. I was grateful.

Though I worked out a careful routine for daily living, bathing remained a chancy affair. When I set out alone for a long hike far from camp and came upon water, I leaped in. Otherwise, I did not bathe. Most men did not. Water was not to be trusted as it often spread disease. General Washington's order was that no man could come on parade with his face or hands dirty. Splashing on a little water from a bucket was sufficient.

Calls of nature were commonly met in the thickets, privately. For fear of the spread of pox and other contagion, the army urged us to use the simple pits near the encampment, but they were foul and disdained by many. So I was not noticeable in my solitary habits. As long as I was alert and aware, I was safe.

Roger and I trained diligently, exercising and drilling and practicing with our weapons. I was secretly delighted that I was as good a shot as he was. All those years hunting with the Thomas boys had trained me well. We had our jokes, our competitions, and sometimes, our arguments.

He played the flute masterfully, favoring Scottish airs and country dances that set us all whistling or humming. I whittled chess pieces and he constructed a hinged collapsible board. The flute and chess were for the quiet hours.

We were part of a small group of rangers quartered near Tarrytown for scouting. Secretly encamped in this countryside indefinitely, our job was to spy on the enemy's movements and bring back intelligence. We moved about furtively, capturing Tories and gathering information. Our missions were manifold; General Washington needed to know what the British planned for the upper Hudson. Fresh daily intelligence was the key to survival for ourselves and for our army.

It was necessary to be prepared every minute. Constant small skirmishes occurred and no place was safe. I acquitted myself well a number of times, not always heroically but satisfactorily.

Once, I was alone in the woods answering a call of nature, when I heard suspicious crackling and rustling above me. I recovered myself quickly and fixed my clothing just in time for an enormous Tory to tumble from an overhanging bough behind me. It was no wonder the branches gave way under him.

Fortunately, the man landed on a large boulder and broke his leg; he was such a robust fellow it would have been hard for me to wrestle him into captivity. I tied him up, then slowly walked him—or rather "hopped" him along leaning on me—back to my company. We were both utterly exhausted by that journey.

Captain Webb interviewed me. "What were you doing out in the wood, Shurtliff?"

"I was gathering mushrooms for dinner, sir."

"Well, lad," he said, eyeing the captive, "he's quite a large and poisonous toadstool. You have heart."

Roger found it all hilarious. "Mushrooms?" he gasped in the midst of his laughter. "Mushrooms?"

I thought it pretty funny myself. "What would you have me say?" I challenged him, but he had already moved on to his next subject for teasing.

"Heart? It had nothing to do with you having heart. The monkey saw your bum from the branch and could not resist. He took you for a fellow monkey."

For weeks the mere utterance of either word—*mushroom* or *heart*—brought on laughter.

By some peculiar attuning of minds, Roger and I often had similar thoughts and understandings. It was as if our judgments were honed on the same whetstone. This had never happened to me with anyone before, and it gave me joy.

✳ ✳ ✳

Though this area of New York was supposedly neutral ground, it was really a no-man's-land, with bands of Tory irregulars troubling the local farmers, stealing their livestock and their crops, and commandeering their provisions. Often, women and children—innocent victims, their men gone—were left to starve. Sometimes the Tories even set fire to the colonists' homes. When we saw the night sky turn flaming red, we quickly mounted our horses and rode to the burning farmstead to find Patriots hanging like rag dolls from boughs or to see Loyalists in feathers and paint dashing off into the darkness.

DeLancey's raiders were the worst. Westchester Tories led by James DeLancey, they were known as "cowboys" because of the cattle they stole. They were hardened fighters and merciless on their countrymen.

In this sheltered glen, Roger and I argued often about war. I believed war was necessary at times, but Roger felt there *always* had to be a better way. He was adamantly opposed to war and would go all the way back to the ancient Greeks to talk about Helen of Troy and foolish wars.

In October the first anniversary of the great battle of Yorktown occurred. I vividly recalled those days in Middleborough, when victory teetered between redcoat and Patriot. Then, I could not contain my excitement and followed the accounts carefully, reading every word I could find about the battle. I recounted my frenzy to Roger.

Then we won and the Patriots forced Cornwallis to surrender! In those days, I could think of nothing else. At my spinning wheel I envisioned the grandeur of the victory, the magnificent final scene: trumpets and swords, triumphant Patriots generous champions in victory.

At first, Roger teased me lightly. "Where did you get these romantic ideas?" he asked, and laughed. He kept up his comments and I began to mind. "Our side won," I reminded him. "Aren't you glad?"

"Of course. But that doesn't change the brutality of it."

Things got tense between us. Finally, he proposed a deal. "I'll let you be. I won't say another word about Yorktown," he vowed, "if you'll promise never to go on about the glorious victory."

Oddly, that very promise he exacted proved to be a

kind of shield for me because, to mark the anniversary, an anonymous broadside bitterly presented a candid look back. This document revealed that Yorktown hadn't been so glorious at all. It argued forcefully as it presented these truths: It was the French, and not the Patriots, who had forced the surrender, because there weren't many Patriots left ready to fight in Yorktown. Many were dead, many wounded, and the rest, starving, ragged, and unpaid, had simply picked up and gone home.

In fact, at Yorktown, while a military band played "The World Turn'd Upside Down," seven thousand British troops slow-marched across the green to drop their arms, slamming the guns down intentionally hard so that they broke.

The great Cornwallis never appeared; he was taken conveniently ill, so General O'Hara of the Guards was sent to surrender in his place. O'Hara blundered and mistakenly tried to surrender to the French general on the field. Embarrassed, he was turned around and pointed the right way.

And, finally, General Washington did not accept the surrender. General Lincoln accepted for Washington: a substitute surrendering to another substitute. To me, all of this greatly reduced the glory.

Nevertheless, the British had lost at Yorktown.

I could not forget that afterward had come news passed by word of mouth of their fearful atrocities. A pregnant woman bayoneted to death in her bed left with her breasts cut open and the message scrawled upon the drapes: THOU SHALT NEVER GIVE BIRTH TO A REBEL. A perfectly formed baby torn from the womb and hung upon a bush. A fourteen-year-old girl raped and left unclad in the street. A Patriot farmer hanged from his own apple tree and tagged with the message: HANGING IS GOOD ENOUGH FOR REBELS. Any second thoughts I'd had about my own false enlistment were erased by these horror stories.

I did not discuss my disillusionment with Roger because we had agreed not to talk about the war. But I knew that he believed I'd been foolish about the romance of it. I was grateful for his silence. He cared enough about my feelings not to crow.

We did all our cooking and eating together. If Roger shot a bird or a rabbit he'd give it to me to cook, because

I knew the wild herbs and the edible mushrooms well and could flavor food so that it was tasty. He took to teasing, "You'd make someone a good wife, Bobby," as a compliment. I laughed, but the remark was too dangerously close to home to be fun. On spying missions and in dangerous situations, we paired off and backed each other up. We knew each could trust the other, and that was precious knowledge.

But always, the great black pit, the lie, lay as a chasm between us, and we remained conditional friends, each with his own secrets. That was the only kind of friend I could have.

There were rumors all the time of a final peace, but General Washington's orders stated, "The readiest way to promote lasting and honorable peace is to be fully prepared vigorously to prosecute war." In Westchester the Tories were very much at war with us still, and we had to be ready.

The winter months were fierce. I now wore woolen breeches and a buckskin waistcoat. My socks were no longer cotton but thick wool. I tied bands of leather around my lower legs to keep them warm, and on very cold days I used sheaves of dry leaves as insulation between the leather strips and the socks. I had never known such cold. The childhood Sundays that I had shivered through in the Middleborough Congregational-ist Church were tropical memories as compared to this.

In winter, things were quieter and one tended to feel safer. We lived now not in tents but closeted in tiny, windowless huts: no privacy, no quiet, very little light. One frigid afternoon there was a call for volunteers for a twenty-man scouting party in the neutral territory near Peekskill Hollow.

"I'm going to go," I told Roger. "I can't bear being cooped up here. I won't be any colder than I am now and at least it will be more lively outdoors."

"I'm with you," he said, and so we volunteered.

We rode out into the woods and it was immediately more lively. As if on signal, we were ambushed by Tories on horseback. The exchange of fire was swift and spir-ited, and they retreated. We had no casualties, which was marvelous good luck, for we'd been outnumbered, but we were freezing and needed rest.

We headed for a nearby house, the only possible refuge in sight.

There we stopped, and the Widow Hunt, a large

woman of fifty or so years with several chins and a bosom surely equal to my father's cousin Captain Simeon Sampson's great pillows, said she was perfectly willing to let us rest there for some hours. In her fireplace was a gorgeous blazing fire that thawed our frozen limbs.

"I will send my slave, George, for food and drink," this agreeable widow offered, and so she promptly did.

She was too nice, too friendly, too willing. I was very restive. There was the shade of dishonesty in her words and her manner. She was catching us with honey. Softly, I confided my fears to Roger.

"Oh, but it's such a great fire!" he groaned. He studied my face intently. "You're sure, Bobby?"

"How can I be sure? I don't think the Widow Hunt is telling the truth. I think she sent George to trap us. It's just a strong feeling I have."

"Then that's enough for me," Roger whispered, and we went together to the sergeant.

"We will leave at once," the sergeant said crisply, and immediately ordered the men to put on their outer garments. He heeded neither the widow's protests nor the men's grumbling. "That's an order. Change of plans. Prepare to depart."

As we moved away from the house, we saw George coming across the icy ground, hands empty.

"Where are the supplies?" the sergeant asked.

"What supplies, suh?"

"The food and drink you were sent for."

George shook his head. "Widow sent me to tell her friends she had some rebels in her house." He surely had no great loyalty to his owner.

"Come along with us," the sergeant ordered.

George had no choice, but he seemed most willing, even delighted. He knew the land and its shortcuts and dangers, and he directed us.

We were right on the bank of the Croton River when in the distance we glimpsed a group of about sixty mounted Tories approaching. We had an unfortunate set of choices: drown in the deep river or be shot by the enemy.

"There's a shallow place—a sandbar—so's the water's not too high," George said. "We can walk across."

"Show us," the sergeant ordered, and we followed George right into the icy river, muskets held high above our heads. When I was almost across, a sudden heavy current swept me off the sandbar and I thrashed about, helpless, in the freezing water. I was nearly drowned by the time Roger somehow managed to throw me a rope and, with help, I was pulled ashore, a cake of ice.

Quickly we thanked George, who had truly saved us, and told him how grateful we were. We had to get to shelter and warmth.

"I'd like to come along and be free," he said.

"Sorry. We can't take you," the sergeant explained. "You belong to the Widow Hunt. We can't take her property."

George nodded, an agonized little smile on his face. He understood; he had been someone's property all his life.

I thought of Jennie and felt so sad.

"Will she punish you for helping us?" Roger asked.

George shook his head. "No, suh. I been with her since I was a boy, so I know how to manage." He turned and headed back.

Silently, except for the chattering of my teeth, we watched him go.

"Someday in this land it will be against the law for people to own other people," Roger whispered fervently.

"Soon?" I wondered.

"Ah, Bobby, when are you going to learn? Nothing is ever soon. That is, no good thing is ever soon enough. Like peace—or the fire we need right now. Let's make haste." He propelled me to move faster.

The sporadic bitter skirmishes continued all through the fierce winter. Three times, men from our group were brutally slain by the enemy. Three boys, really—I barely knew them, yet Roger and I broke the frozen sod and spaded and dug their graves, then shoveled the earth atop their coffins and stood next to the bare, stony mounds that were once brave young men.

One night, after such a grim burial detail, while we were splashing at the water bucket washing off the mud and grime, I protested, "It makes no sense, Roger. The war is long over."

The grizzled veteran next to Roger, who never called me by name but always mocked my youth, answered me. "It is—all over but the killin', baby face. All over but the dyin'." Then he spat a glob of tobacco juice into the dust and laughed raucously.

What he said seemed horribly so.

Winter crept on and then spring, with its kinder

weather, passed in this endless, pointless local fighting and waiting.

At the beginning of June, we enjoyed one long, oddly quiet interlude, and on a gentle, sunlit afternoon as we were playing chess, Roger stretched lazily and said, "This is my kind of war: no big battles, no attacks. If we could just stay here helping the locals and sneaking around spying to discover what Tommy Lobster is up to, I'd sign up again."

"Ah, Roger, you're dreaming. This is just a lull."

"I'm not the dreamer. Look at the board. Mate!" he declared triumphantly.

It was so; I had been preoccupied. I began to gather up the chessmen. "I sense trouble coming," I confessed. "I've a premonition."

"What?" He made light of it. "What are you, a woman?"

Dear God. Say yes to that! Nod silent assent. Now is the time to tell him, to speak the truth. Though my mind urged honesty, my tongue was heavy as a brick in my mouth.

"Why do you call me that?"

"Because it is women who have premonitions. You lost a little chess game, and that turned you into Deborah the prophet?"

Startled, I searched his face but could see only candor

there. He just knew his Bible well—it was an innocent remark. Still, the forewarning lay heavy on my mind. Danger lurked near. Perhaps I did sense it because I *was* a woman, or perhaps because I was a liar, or perhaps because of both.

The summer night was hot and I remained wide awake and anxious. After several difficult hours of forcing myself to lie still, I rose, mindful that the others were sleeping. I sneaked out of the tent. The moon guided me down the steep, rocky path to the fresh pond set low in the maple swamp. A swim in the clear, cool water would refresh me and relieve my feverish fears.

Quickly, I divested myself of my clothes, placing them beneath a thick bush, and plunged into the still water. I swam briskly at first, then lay back to float in the deep center and ponder my dilemma once again. *He will have to be told. It gets harder and harder as the days pass. He trusts me. I cannot keep lying to him.*

Suddenly there was a small noise on shore, a rustling amid the shrubbery. A nocturnal animal no doubt. I stayed very still and listened, then tried to peer in the direction on the bank from whence it came.

A soldier stood there, his white leggings bright in the darkness.

*The night watch? He's usually posted up on the perimeter. What
is he doing down here? Oh Lord!*

"Ah, there you are, Bobby," Roger whispered.

I was stricken.

"Do not come into the water," I begged.

"What? You would keep this coolness to yourself
on this hot night? Some friend you are!" He was already
pulling off his leggings.

"Roger, go back to the tent. Go back!"

It was too late.

"Here I come. Prepare for a ducking."

He stood atop the great craggy rock, his beautiful
long, lean body outlined in the moonlight. Then he
poised himself and dived cleanly into the pool. He
stayed under until he emerged directly in front of me,
grabbing me around the shoulders playfully.

For a second he held on to me, his arm crooked
firmly under my chin, and as our bodies touched I felt
the shock hit him and his manhood stiffen. He gasped
and let out an eerie, strangled cry: "Bobby!"

"I can explain—I was going to tell—" I blubbered.

He forced my head up and looked into my eyes, then
kissed me violently. Then he lifted his face away an inch.
"In the name of God, how could you—?"

"Who's out there?" an angry voice challenged from the shore. "Friend or foe?"

This time it *was* the night watch.

"Identify yourself." He had his musket at the ready.

"Friend. Roger Snow. Put down the gun." Roger abruptly pushed me away and struck out swiftly toward the guard. I moved deep underwater, heading away as quietly as possible in the opposite direction.

Hiding doesn't matter anymore, I told myself even as I moved. *Roger will have to tell him. Then he'll summon the others and they'll form the gauntlet so that the drum can beat the whore's march for naked Deborah Sampson, at last.*

I floated in the water, inert, delaying the terrible moment. There were no further sounds on shore. Still, I waited some time more.

Finally, trembling and terrified, I climbed out, trying to cover my body with my hands.

There was no one about.

He could have turned me in—but he didn't do it. He was furious and he had every right to be. Somehow he managed to save me. Now I don't have to tell him. He knows. He must care for me a lot to forgive me, to protect me like this. He didn't turn me in! He must love me!

There was this one moment of pure, hysterical happiness—then I reached for my clothes. My breeches were gone. I searched around. My other garments lay in the pile where I'd left them, but my breeches were gone.

Shamed and miserable, I understood. Roger, no matter how hurt and angry, could not bring himself to turn me in. He was incapable of it. To be viciously vindictive was against his nature.

So he used my false costume, the breeches, as a way of marking my cowardice. He used the lie I was living. *Here, liar, the breeches are a symbol of what you are.*

If only he still lay awake in the tent and I could get him up and outside, we could talk. Then I could explain. . . .

I dressed in what clothing I had left, wearing the jacket and using its tails to wrap my lower body, and I crept through the dark woods back to the tent. On my pillow, legs knotted as if to prohibit any further wear, lay the breeches. I forced the knots open quickly and donned them.

On his cot, Roger was a concealed mound completely buried beneath his blanket. I resolved: *I will talk to him in the morning. I will tell him my whole story. He will listen. He will forgive the give-away child and he will understand.*

I lay impatiently awaiting dawn. *He's a good man, a sensible, kind fellow. He did not reveal my secret. He will listen. Daylight will bring understanding.*

Instead, daylight brought DeLancey's raiders, who came down upon us like wolves on the fold.

5. The Solitary Rider

The raiders descended before daybreak in a quick and ferocious charge. There was not a moment to think. I'd read so much about warfare, but at that moment I knew nothing. I barely had time to grab my gun in the semi-darkness as we scrambled to defend ourselves.

This was heavy combat, real war at last!

I reacted at first excitedly when I heard the thunder of many pounding horses' hooves and the shouts of the enemy. No different from the men around me, I was filled with the delirium of war.

I had been in the army all these many months performing various quiet duties and surviving minor frays, and this was my baptism in battle warfare. Not one-on-one in a lonely spot but all of us gloriously engaged.

I was thrilled by the violent sounds, the shouts of men in turmoil, the pandemonium of men in struggle.

But I did not enjoy combat—unlike so many of the veterans I'd listened to who'd gloried in and relived what they had done first to this enemy, then to that one, reenacting bloody feats. I fought without hesitation or thought. I fired rounds in unison with my comrades, and stabbed and scuffled with my foes. I soon had a bloody bayonet because I did what a soldier had to do.

And because I wanted to survive.

Worst of the morning's woes was the clear glimpse I'd got of Roger, his tunic slashed and his shoulder bleeding, pinned against a rock by an unsteady Tory lad who held a saber.

As I watched, Roger suddenly writhed to his right, deftly extricating himself, and shot his foe straight through the heart. Then as the Tory crumpled to the ground, I saw Roger drop to his knees to cradle his dead enemy's head and weep while all about him the battle raged. Only the smoke and havoc of DeLancey's raiders' onslaught spared him somehow from the horses' hooves and the perilous hail of bullets.

A dozen hurt, five dead out of our small company. Nine of the enemy killed.

I had never dreamed that war could be so terrible. Deacon and Mistress Thomas and other elders had often warned me to beware of my uncommonly rich imagination. "It comes from your head being too much in the books," the deacon scolded. "Such an imagination in a woman can only lead to trouble."

Reality this day had beggared that imagination.

I was not brave, but I knew now I'd do anything to stay alive. I'd learned this the moment I speedily clipped my bayonet on the point of my gun and drew blood.

Once, while hunting, I was charged by a wild boar, and another time I was nearly stomped by an angry buck, but I had never before been surrounded by enraged men powered by hate, lusting to take my life. *I want to live!* my brain screamed, over and over. I didn't think about anything else as I fought desperately. Only that: *I want to live!*

Right after the Tories had retreated—even before the Patriots' wounds were dressed or the dead gathered off the ground—our captain, his arm broken, the bone jutting up through his sleeve at the elbow like a roasted turkey drumstick, ordered his battered men to assemble.

"They're not gone," Captain Webb said. He lay on the ground, pale enough to be his own ghost, his back propped on a rock. "Men, the Tories have pulled back only to regroup. The bastards know how few we are and, mark me, they'll be back. You gave 'em hell. General Washington himself would raise a glass to you. But we won't be able to stop them next time. We need help.

"I want a volunteer—to ride west immediately to summon Colonel Sproat and his men, who are camped near the river."

He waited.

Colonel Sproat? Was he the same Sproat who kept the tavern in Middleborough? I'd carried butter and eggs there on errands. I'd measured my height in his doorway dozens of times. It was his copy of *Common Sense* I'd read after the deacon slapped me and forbade it.

"Who'll go? Who will bring word to Colonel Sproat? I need a courier—who will travel with the wings of Mercury." Captain Webb was a former schoolmaster, occasionally given to such elegant phrases.

Only birds' songs broke the silence.

Dismayed, he looked around.

There was an uncomfortable shifting of feet. The men did not return his gaze. They stood at ease, their eyes cast downward or into the far distance. Each knew what was being proposed: a perilous daylight journey through Tory country. He was asking for a volunteer for a one-way ride, for a suicide mission.

"Damn it!" Captain Webb could not believe what he saw. "I would go myself if I could stay on a mount! Is there no one here man enough to volunteer?"

Unaccountably, my feet moved forward.

Courage? No, quite the opposite: madness, the madness of despair. I'd had enough. My personal cowardice with Roger had been sufficient for this lifetime. He was wounded but he would never let me near to help him; I could help him and my comrades best by going. I would forsake this life now. Perhaps this way I could leave it honorably.

I had not meant to step up nor had I intended to say the words that next came forth from my mouth. "I will go to Colonel Sproat," I heard my own voice promise. "I will bring help."

"You're just a lad, but you have courage. I saw you do

combat today that would make your mother proud,"
Captain Webb said.

Not my mother, I thought, suppressing a smile. Turning
away quickly, I felt how the captain's praise had brought
both warmth and color to my cheeks.

Roger, limp and pale, winced and closed his eyes as I
volunteered. He obviously could not bear to look on me.

Then I panicked. What if he told? They would never
send a woman on this mission. But I knew he would not.

He raised his hands to stop his ears.

Well, you will never have need to hear me or look on me again,
I thought. Resolutely, I turned away and moved off to
make myself ready.

Now I was the courier—I liked the word. It had been
used for Paul Revere.

I was a solitary rider moving stealthily through dangerous territory. "Careful, Mercury. Careful." Softly, I
urged my horse on faster and faster through those same
green woods and fields of Westchester in the brilliant
light of the June afternoon. "Careful," I whispered one
more time, but it was more a caution to myself than to
the horse.

I still drew comfort from the childhood habit,

learned in Widow Thacher's lonely house, of talking to myself. "How could my life be so complicated?" I murmured miserably in the silent woods. "How could I be so doomed?"

The horse followed the twisted path, with me squinting into the glare over the high brush and peering up at the great firs and oaks, aware that death rustled amid their greenness.

I was on a death mission, traveling without papers or identification so that if I were ambushed here no one would ever know and I would dissolve into the carpet of the forest. "Take heed or you'll soon be compost," I reminded myself. I loved the forest, loved to wander amid its grasses, mushrooms, birds, and small animals, but I had no desire to nourish it.

I knew I could as easily die in those woods as I'd seen my comrades die, with less notice. I'd witnessed my share of military funerals. After a few pious words and a slow, melancholy stanza on a bugle, the living closed ranks quickly. Just like that, I could disappear and the world would take little notice.

My mind kept repeating the bitter truth: *But the war is not over yet.*

I spurred my horse.

Alert, rifle in hand, I hunched low in the saddle seeking out small telltale signs on the trail. I was reassured by the sight of a doe and her fawns drinking at a stream, and by an occasional startled raccoon or woodchuck darting away into the woods. Other riders had not recently come this way.

My mind often turned to Roger, but I forced myself to stop those thoughts and concentrate on my vital errand. Still, that moment in the water floated into memory again and again. I found my fingers on my lips tracing his kiss.

My throat was parched and several times I almost gave in to the ravaging thirst, for I carried a full canteen of water in my saddlebag. But I knew better than to drink. I had little reprimands stored in my brain that I gave myself during the various calls of nature. For thirst: To drink now, Deborah, means the need to stop to pass water later, and for that you will have to squat in some open space in daylight.

Then either some Tories or Tommy Lobster or, worst of all, my own comrades would discover me, and my secret would be revealed. Oh, to be able to urinate standing up! How many thousands of times in my army career I had that wistful thought!

I did not drink.

I was accustomed to finding my way in the woods, and the captain's directions were clear. Several times I dismounted to kneel and study the grassy tract, but it was intact. When a pair of hawks circled overhead, swooping and diving, I was glad of their company. I tried to listen to everything: the lapping of the water, the rustling of the wind. I sniffed for smoke; my eyes sought traps or any clues of the enemy.

On one of these stops, beside a pond, I decided to just wet my mouth with the clear, cold water, then spit it out. I lay down on the mossy bank near a bush abutting some rocks and leaned my head over so that I could taste the lovely water. Just wet your mouth, I warned myself. Don't swallow. Not a drop.

I opened my mouth, and in the still, mirrored reflection I saw to one side of me a copperhead, his reddish little head gleaming in the bright sun. I knew he saw me. I stared him down, not even blinking my eyes or turning my head. I stayed rigid and tried to still my breathing. I know copperheads; if you scare them, they attack and they're swift. They don't look for trouble, but if they think *you're* looking for trouble—well, watch out. Mostly, a copperhead bite kills.

I lay there sweating, still as an old fallen log, till the snake slid away.

I guess it wasn't long, only a half hour or so, but it felt long and I reproached myself for this delay. My thirst was a fault. A soldier can't give in to thirst that way. I wondered if men thirsted as much.

Now I made Mercury fly for me! Maybe the Tories would need to do some heavy sleeping after their night's marauding; I hoped so. Two hours of hard riding brought me within sight of Colonel Sproat's encampment.

An incredible joy filled me as I raced my tired horse into their midst, my hat low over my face and a handkerchief shielding my nose and mouth from the dust. "Captain Webb needs help," I panted, and Colonel Sproat was immediately at my side.

"Make ready, men, while I hear the particulars," the colonel ordered. "We go at once." He glanced up at me and there was no flicker of recognition. The crisis, the uniform, the short hair, the male stance, and the deep, soft voice had transformed me. I was no longer the deacon's bond servant, who came on errands from the farm. Colonel Sproat never would have dreamed such a wild thing. Now he listened attentively to my account of the attack.

"You will not find us lacking," he assured me. "Neither will the Tories. Take a fresh mount. Well done, soldier."

Weary though I was, I was buoyed by the colonel's praise and the sudden, fresh hope that this rescue party might save Roger and the others. I might yet get to explain. Thus is hope born and reborn after it dies.

I led my horse off to the meadow. Patting the loyal animal's sweaty face, I whispered, "You get to stay here and rest, Mercury." I slipped a thong with a makeshift wooden nameplate with *Mercury* scratched on it onto the horse's rope. I was eager to be back with my comrades, but I was nonetheless wistful as I left my mount. "You don't know how lucky you are being born a horse. It beats being born a girl."

The return ride was much faster and happier, because I was bringing help and because there were many courageous men galloping alongside me. As we approached Captain Webb's troop, we began to hear the shot and rumble of battle and to smell the gunpowder. Above the din rose gray, whirling plumes of smoke. DeLancey's raiders had not wasted any time.

Colonel Sproat's tactic was to divide our troops into three even wedges, each to descend from an unexpected angle. At his signal, we Patriots galloped down into the besieged camp, shooting and yelling like Indians— confounding the enemy so that our strength could not be estimated.

Fighting on horseback, I was futilely looking about for Roger when I felt a sudden sting in my left thigh near the groin, as if a bee were inside my flesh. I slipped to the side and was nearly heaved off. I held on dearly, swaying in the saddle. A musket ball, I knew. I understood then that I would die there. Oddly, I was thrilled, for I saw that the Tories had been surprised by the reinforcements and were being routed in brutal battle.

One more volley brought an even sharper pain to my lower left leg, and my breeches were instantly sticky. I had never known such searing agony as the horse jounced and jarred me, driving the pain deeper within. Still, I managed to stay on my mount and fight.

The Tories outnumbered us, but our ferocity at last

won the day. We watched in weary relief as the enemies'
horses turned in retreat.

In that very last second, an angry Tory madly flailing
his saber slashed my brow, blinding me in the flow of
my own warm blood. I tumbled from my mount, landing next to a dead Tory whose head had been split open
like a melon.

The bearded veteran who so liked to tease me dismounted and ran over. "We must get you to a doctor."

"No. Just leave me be." I hated the thought of a hospital. I had pledged to myself that I would die first. I
feared disclosure and disgrace far more than death.

"A head wound is serious, lad."

"Don't touch me. Save yourself with the others lest
the Tories come back. Leave me here. I am going to die."
I closed my eyes, my body stiff with pain, and longed for
blissful unconsciousness.

"I'll hear no more," he persisted, and with the captain's permission he hoisted my body onto his horse and
tied me securely, then set off at a rapid pace for a farmhouse eight miles away that had been turned into a medical station.

I remember nothing of that journey. My first
thought on coming to, as the horse carried me, was of

suicide. But my guardian must have been a dairy farmer, for he knew how to truss an animal for transport. Each of my hands had been separately roped into a handcuff and then securely tied to my body. There was no way I could get to my pistol tied up as I was. "I can't go to a hospital," I moaned over and over into the horse's flank. "I took a vow."

"There, there, Bobby. You're out of your blinkin' head. We'll soon be there and we'll get help."

It was the first time he'd ever called me respectfully by a real name.

I knew there was nothing to be done.

The place was filled with the maimed victims of the Tories. I lay on a mat in the large open area watching the surgeon, whose specialty seemed to be bullet extraction. First, a nurse would hastily disrobe the injured man or in severe cases just cut away the clothing around the wound; then two assistants would hold down the patient while the doctor grasped a silver probe, slightly curved at the end, and inserted it into the wound, moving it about till he forced out the shot. Each turn of the probe would bring groans or shouts of pain and often a convulsion. The bullet hole would then be cleansed and bandaged afterward.

Never! I resolved. *I'll die before I let him dig into me that way.* I was determined even though I could not shut out the pictures of untreated gangrenous wounds: sores, running pus, scabs, flies. My injuries would surely become infected. And then what? No matter. Either way, this was the end. Vainly, I tugged at the cloth of my breeches so that the bullet holes were less visible.

"What have we here?" the surgeon asked.

"A cut to my head, sir."

"Is that all?"

"Yes, sir."

The doctor washed my bloody brow with soap and water, then disinfected it with brandy, spilling some. Little tongues of fire licked at my forehead.

"You are very pale. You have lost a quantity of blood, soldier. Let's get right at this." The doctor tendered me a full glass of brandy. "We've little laudanum and we need what we have for the amputations," he explained. Since he was watching me closely, I figured it was wise to take a large sip of the brandy. Unaccustomed to gulping such strong drink, I unfortunately suffered an explosion of coughs. "Swallow it all," the doctor urged. "It kills the pain."

He began to probe at the wound. "'Tis not so deep as a well, nor so wide as a church door," he muttered.

"'But 'tis enough, 'twill serve,'" I responded, and at the doctor's startled glance I said, "I taught school last year and learned the lines."

The doctor sloshed some more spirits on the injury to keep it sterile and finally applied a salve and bandages. "Go into the small room next door and take off your clothing. We will examine you for other wounds."

"I have no others, sir. Just the head."

The doctor gave me a penetrating look. "You've lost much blood." His eyes caught sight of the bullet hole in the thigh of the breeches. "Wait. What is that from?"

"A faulty tack in the saddle. I suffered only a scratch, but it tore the cloth. I'm very weary. If I might rest for a while, I'll be fine." My fatigue was genuine, but the innocence in my manner was feigned.

The doctor, accustomed to malingerers and to men who imagined their wounds much graver than they were, waved his hand granting permission. "Sit here for a few minutes, and when you're steady you may go in and lie down on the cot." He moved on to a soldier in the far corner calling out piteously that the toes on his left foot were cramping, and he needed a liniment rub. He had no feet; both legs had been amputated at the knees.

I sat motionless until all the interest in the room was focused on the poor fellow in the corner. Then I rose clumsily, supporting myself by clutching a heavy shelf with one hand, while with the other I stealthily helped myself from the medical cabinet to bandages, lint, a pot of the salve, and one of the silver probes. My pain was so intense I believe I might have made off with precious laudanum, but there was none in sight. I had to make do with a small flask of brandy. Only then did I find my way into the bare little room that must once have been a pantry, where I lay down upon the cot. By hoisting my good leg up against the wall, I forced myself into a most uncomfortable position so that I would remain awake. After I rested a short while in this manner, I rose.

I slipped out like a thief—indeed, I was a thief, for I'd tucked my ill-gotten supplies into a thin blanket and knotted it. I had always been careful to take only what was mine, but there was no help for it now. War changed all the rules. The bullets in my leg had to be removed. I managed to creep on all fours like an old dog to a thicket alongside a stream, where I lay all night dozing fitfully, waiting for the morning light so that I could attempt surgery on myself.

How I wished I had the laudanum. There was not sufficient brandy to numb me, though I shook the very last of it into my mouth and inserted my little finger like a cork to swab out the neck of the flask and then lick the precious drops. I examined my thigh. The bleeding was now intermittent. The hole was large, about a half inch in diameter. Seizing the small probe, I plunged it in brutally, digging deep to force out the bullet. The pain was fiery. Still the bullet did not emerge. Panting, I probed and pushed, and this time my own screams of anguish rang loud in my ears; yet I needed to persist, no matter the pain. Once I saw the extricated bloody ball roll out and drop on the mossy bank, I fainted and fell atop it.

Much later, I examined my leg and saw that the second musket ball was deeply embedded. I was too weak to attempt its removal; it would be a permanent lodger. If I survived, I'd have to learn to live with it.

Foraging, scouring the countryside for mushrooms and berries, dandelions and purslane, an occasional game bird, fish, and one blessed rabbit, I managed to stay in hiding. Caves and great rocks were my nightly shelters as I waited out the slow, painful healing until I could walk unsupported by a stick. After ten days of hiding in the woods, I came across members of my regiment return-ing from a scouting mission. They hailed me with joy—they'd thought me dead.

I had learned much; I now knew how thoroughly I despised war. The great adventure and glory of it were the corrupted visions of men. I had been misled somehow and wandered willingly into the dreams of strangers.

I could have deserted.

But I had enlisted for the duration and accepted the sixty pounds' bounty money. My love for my country and its dream of independence was not diminished. The Tories, our hateful enemies, had to be driven from our shores.

So I went back to West Point because that was where I belonged.

It never occurred to me to do anything else.

6. The Confession

The saber slash on my brow was superficial and mended quickly, but the bullet wounds oozed, then crusted and stubbornly would not close. Each day's field exercises started the bleeding anew, and afterward I sometimes hobbled about clumsily. I feared my leg injuries would be discovered once there was a long march. I continued to wear the bandage on my head, pretending that the saber wound needed care and that was what affected my walking and balance.

Others in my group were far worse off. And the weakest man, alas, was my beloved Roger, who neither spoke to nor looked at me. The day after I came back, I screwed my courage to the sticking point and approached him. "Roger, let me explain," I whispered.

"Stop!" he rebuffed me so loudly that others turned to stare. I tried again several times, privately, but he simply turned away. If he was resting or reading, he closed his eyes and would not hear me. He was resolute in his indifference to me.

Oddly, though he wore no bandages and bore no visible marks of injury, he was increasingly unsteady. He, who had been so lithe and graceful at enlistment, moved now with the hesitant gait of an unsure old man fearful of falling. It was as if he had some deep, unhealed wound that was sapping his strength. I didn't know what injuries he'd received in the attack, but I suspected that, whatever else the cause, killing the Tory lad had devastated him. For Roger it was as if, in shooting the boy in the heart, he'd put a bullet in his own.

A fortnight after my return, the dreaded order for a long march came and our group set out. I managed to limp along, though in pain. I kept my eyes wistfully on Roger, who was wobbling two rows up ahead of me. *Step,* I willed him to walk. *Step, step, step!* After several miles, I saw him stumble, and instead of recovering, he crumpled to the ground.

The corporal ran to him. "Resume ranks," he

ordered the men who had milled around. Kneeling, he put his hand to Roger's brow. "He is burning with fever. He can't go with us," the corporal determined. "He must stop here."

I was frantic. Roger could not be left behind. I needed to talk to him, to explain. I grasped desperately for a way that might save him and help myself as well. I pointed to a nearby prosperous-looking farmhouse.

"I will stay and take care of him," I volunteered. "I am not yet fully well myself." My hand moved to my head bandage. "Once he's better, we'll join up with the rest of you." This respite would give me a chance to talk to him. He would have to listen. It would also give my own leg wounds a chance to heal. "That is, if the farmer will have us."

"Oh, he can't say no. This is neutral territory. This farmer will surely help two wounded Continental soldiers," the corporal said airily. He didn't want his troop to be delayed, so he embraced the idea. "It's his patriotic duty."

While we all knew this was neutral ground, we also knew there was still fierce guerrilla fighting here, and the king's supporters were a constant danger.

"Soon as this citizen sees Snow's condition, he'll

offer to take him in," the corporal said, ordering two of the men to carry Roger to the ornate front door. There, we were received by a fat, dour Dutchman. He looked as though he'd never passed up a dish at table.

"You own this place, Mr. . . . ?" inquired the corporal.

"William Van Tassel. Yes, this is my property."

"We have two wounded Patriots here. One is very sick." He indicated Roger and waited. "They need rest for a few days," he went on, unabashed. "We will leave them here with you."

Patriotic duty? I thought, marking the landlord's hostile stance. *He never had such a thought in his life.*

There was a long pause. Van Tassel didn't blink. He stared down the corporal.

We're trapped, I realized. *This man does not want us here, but Roger cannot go on.*

Both Van Tassel and the corporal were masters of the waiting game. Van Tassel could hardly refuse outright. His sympathies might have been Tory, but his property was in the Patriots' domain. So, in the end, he had to give way. "Bring him in" was his surly concession.

Once the soldiers were gone and the inside door locked, he curtly bade me, "Come," and I followed him, weighed down by the unconscious body on my shoulder.

My bad leg buckled several times as we climbed up the two steep flights of stairs, and I had to hug the banister to stay upright while holding on to Roger. It was a balancing act carried on behind the enormous buttocks of the master of the house. I passed portraits of ugly Van Tassel ancestors with whiskers growing back near their ears, staring disdainfully at me. Not a single woman ancestor did I spy, only whiskers. Finally we were in the attic, a bare, filthy warren of tiny rooms.

"My companion has a high fever and is very sick," I appealed. "Must he lie on a dirty wooden floor? Isn't it possible to find a bed for him downstairs in this big house?"

"The hospitality of this house is limited in wartime. I am not running an inn. The attic floor is good enough for rebels" was the rejoinder. My heart sank at the words, which had the echo of the Yorktown taunts: *Good enough for rebels.*

"Here's the lantern. In the corner is a bucket of water. Beside it is the chamber pot. Set it on the top stair at night and the servant will empty it. You have all you will need," our gracious host said. "Feel free to depart as soon as you are able. You understand that when you leave here, you will forget anything you heard or saw. I have many friends all over Westchester who care about my good name. Remember that."

He departed, providing us with neither food nor drink.

I lay down on the floor in despair next to my beloved, helpless comrade. His sensitive face was gaunt, his forehead hot. My own throat was raw with thirst. And I was uneasy. Van Tassel was a Tory, of course. That was what his parting words warned. The Dutchman meant us no good. Perhaps he was planning to let us starve up there? Or to turn us over to a Tory band? Or to kill us? Like anonymous death in the forest, death in this house would go unreported. Who would know?

After many hours, a tap at the attic door panicked me. I opened the door a crack and first inhaled a heavy, sweet scent, and then saw what seemed to be a vision: a young woman of about my own age! A friend? My heart leaped. Plump, and pretty, with a round face and long blond hair. "I am Katharina Van Tassel, daughter to William."

I opened the door.

"Father says I am to bring you only what's left in the kitchen."

"I am sorry to give you extra chores," I said. "Blame it on the war."

"Oh, I don't mind," she said with a grin. "Life is dull here. The war makes it interesting. I don't care about politics. That's men's business. But I do like company."

She came in. "Here is fish chowder and cheese and a sip of wine." She took the lid off the bowl, which held a few teaspoonfuls of chowder, and the scent of that bit of chowder nearly undid me. I covered my face with my hands to conceal tears of gratitude. I had never been so hungry. When I found voice to speak, I said, "I thank you." I held my hands palm-to-palm in prayer position.

Katharina surprised me by stroking my upper arm. "Eat," she said.

"First I must try to feed my friend. He is very ill."

She walked over to gaze at Roger and then suddenly prodded his leg hard with the toe of her elegant black slipper. He did not respond.

"Don't!" I said quickly. "He is desperately sick."

As if she had not heard, in the same brutal manner she then poked the sick man's hip. "He is beyond help," she said. "You'd better eat all that I brought. There's just enough for one. Save yourself."

I shook my head. Grateful for the food, I nevertheless

wished her out. I couldn't believe she'd kicked Roger. I wanted to be alone with him.

"Eat," she urged again.

"Only after I care for my friend." I went to the door and opened it. "Which I must do in private, for it is not a nice sight for a young lady to watch. Thank you for your kindness."

She seemed surprised and unready to leave.

"There are certain uncontrollable bodily needs," I started, and, when she didn't move, I bent down to pick up the chamber pot. "When nature calls, he cannot wait—"

Now she moved toward the door hastily. "I'll bring you supper evenings."

"I'm grateful." With relief, I shut and locked the door and settled down beside him. "Roger," I said, "here is something good to eat. Some nourishment for you." I lifted his head onto my lap and tried to spoon the chowder into his mouth, but it dribbled out. His eyelids fluttered. "Open your eyes," I urged, but either he would not or could not. He took neither food nor drink that night.

Then I gobbled what little soup there was.

As I ate, I wondered at my own bad temper. I was furious with this Katharina. I hated her. Yet she'd brought me food and I was starving. She was probably right about Roger being desperately ill, but I didn't care to hear it from her. I didn't care to hear it said so unfeelingly. I didn't care to hear anything from her.

I needed Roger to live, to stay with me here in this enemy house. I needed to explain about my disguise, about who I really was and why I had not told him. He would understand and forgive me. Maybe he would even love me? He was fond of me. From the very beginning, *he* had chosen to be *my* friend. I had not initiated it; *he* had, for I dared not get close to anyone.

What was it about Katharina? I felt no gratitude even though she'd fed me. She was my only help here and I did not appreciate it. The minute I saw her—in fact, the minute I smelled her before I saw her—I begrudged her all: the perfume, the soft clothes, and the very elegant shoe she used to toe my sick companion. She would look like her father someday, I pictured with satisfaction. She would have bosoms like udders and an arse like her father's.

Probably she had no political opinions; few women did. They were not required of her. "She is the daughter of a Tory," I confided to the silent attic. "I suspect every word she says."

Then I felt a little ashamed of these petty thoughts. Even if she herself was a Tory, she was doing what little there was to do for me. I resolved that I would try to be courteous and more thankful when she returned.

I did try, but no word she could utter pleased me.

"I have added a tidbit Father will not miss," she confided, laughing mischievously, on the third night of our captivity. There was an inch of herring that looked already chewed. Still . . .

I gave her my hand in thanks, and she pressed the hand fervently and held it for a long time. I had my suspicions about the herring having been cleaned off someone's dinner plate, or more likely off the floor because there was a small dust ball garnishing it, but I brushed it off and ate it, hungrily. This time she had brought with her a tapestry cushion, on which she was inclined to sit and watch me eat. "You need company up here. It is unnatural to be so alone."

"I am often alone. It is my nature," I replied, but she tittered at that. Her conversation dwelled on her kitchen trickery, how she had cleverly pilfered a choice bit of cheese and hidden it in her apron pocket and how she had made off with the end sliver of ham. My imprisonment had furnished a delightful new game for her. Once in a while, I'd ask Roger a question, stop to give him a drink, or try to include him in some way. "Don't waste your time on him," she advised.

She sat for so long, to make conversation I asked her if she sometimes read to fill the hours, and if so what did she read?

"Oh, I was done with reading when I finished my schooling. I never read unless I have to," she said, twisting a blond curl on her forefinger, "and it tires the eyes. I do not want to wear spectacles."

I thought, *Aha! I know just the mate for you: Noah Greene. Except that you're not tall enough for him. Your wits, however, are equally dwarfed.*

When I excused myself and rose to feed Roger, hoping she would leave, she said, "I shall look away. But you really need not bother with him, you know. He's a dead man. You'd best eat it all."

I hated that she harped on that. Her words were incredibly cruel. Who knew what Roger could hear or not hear? I withstood these callous comments in silence, though a perilously strong inner voice furnished unspoken responses: *"Shut up! Shut up and go!"*

Chattering on endlessly about the shortages of imported Belgian lace and other such unendurable hardships in a young lady's life these days, she didn't notice that I contributed little conversation.

"You are very brave," she said when at last she got up to leave. "You are a hero and deserve a hero's reward."

"Hardly a hero. Rather I seem to be your father's prisoner."

"And I seem to be your jailer," she said with a merry laugh. "If you should need your jailer suddenly in the night, my room is the one right off the staircase on the first landing. It is always unlocked."

I could not believe the boldness of this invitation. The army had its tavern women and camp followers, so I had witnessed loose behavior before and felt sad for those unfortunate females and their wretched lives. But Katharina was the respectable daughter of a well-off farmer. She had all I had never had and she seemed to make waste of it. I heard her giggling as she descended the stairs, and I wondered that she could find our pitiful plight a laughing matter.

The days passed slowly. We'd been there a week and from the vantage point of the one tiny window, I noted the frequent comings and goings to the farmhouse. In the night I heard noisy arguments downstairs confirming my suspicions: This location was still a Tory stronghold. One evening a rowdy company joined Van Tassel for a drunken party. The Tories were living high on the drink and provisions they stole. The very horses they rode, they boasted, were loot.

I made sure both our muskets were always charged, and I fastened a rope to the ledge of the window should desperate escape be necessary. I kept the attic-room door barred, fearing intruders: drunken Tories or a vengeful host. And I tried to talk to Roger, to gently rouse him and feed him. I spent hours daydreaming about how, when he was well, I would tell him all. I wanted so for him to know me, not as Robert Shurtliff but as Deborah Sampson. But he seemed to be adrift, and elsewhere, already removed from this world.

Katharina must really have liked me because her bounty increased. If the bread had mold, or the potato rotten spots, I ate it all silently. I suspected she was having her fun serving spoiled food; even so there was never enough to chase hunger away. If the food supply was short, her visits were not. Each one, it seemed to me, grew longer. I appreciated the food but grew increasingly nervous. Surely she was needed elsewhere. Surely her father would notice her absences.

She reassured me. "My father is busy with his affairs. He does not think of me." She pouted. "No man ever thinks of me. Do you?"

"Yes. That is, I'm very grateful—"

"I mean think of *me*. Not of your dinner." She laughed harshly. "I am speaking of passion—not food."

"A hungry man's passion is food."

Pressed this way, I was inspired to lie. "Katharina, you should know I am promised to someone."

She looked crestfallen. "But you look so young."

"We have grown up together, she and I."

"What is her name?"

"Deborah Sampson."

"Is she prettier than I am?"

Perhaps not, but taller. My mind supplied the answers mockingly. *And smarter!*

I smiled. "She is very different."

Katharina gave this some thought. "But you may never see her again. She is far from you right now."

"True. But I am pledged, and I must hope."

"You are a strange one," she said. "You spend hours trying to feed a practically dead man. And you are true to a woman you may never see again."

I shrugged.

If anything, this information that I had a girlfriend seemed to whet her appetite. She boldly preferred to sit nearly on top of me. Often she smiled and gazed at me fondly. How dearly I would have loved to have a friend, to receive a kind, friendly human embrace, but I did not want it from her.

I tried to take no notice of her occasional fondling of my arm or my shoulder. She stroked me like a buyer appraising a stallion for purchase. Several times I had to get up and move to sit elsewhere so that our knees and thighs and buttocks would not touch. I pleaded the heat of the room. But then she would move too, saying that she was shortsighted and needed to be close to see me. I understood what it was like to be the fly caught in the spider's web. Why this spider wanted this fly was a mystery to me.

Roger had some good days, when he seemed a bit stronger and took some nourishment and drink, and I rejoiced. But mostly he slept. During his brief wakeful moments, his mind sometimes wandered back to when he was a child in Concord fishing for trout in Walden Pond or blackberrying or sledding in the winter snow. Once he whispered hastily after Katharina knocked,

"She is evil. She has no kindness. She kicked me to see if I was dead."

So he *had* felt and heard her cruelty during those first dreadful days and nights.

He never uttered a word or opened his eyes while Katharina was in our attic room. I suspected he was listening while he feigned sleep to avoid her. Would that I, too, could have done that.

I ministered to him gladly, like a nurse, sponge-bathing him when the fever was high and caring for his wasted body as gently as I could. Cruel scars cross-hatched on his neck and chest, inflicted by the Tory, were livid but not festering. Several times, I told him where we were and what our plight was, but he did not respond. I had no idea what he understood.

It was as if that strange night in the pond had never happened. No words about it passed between us, and I did not dare to broach the subject.

On a Saturday night, for some Tory reason, Van Tassel had a long, loud party, and the next evening Katharina brought us a dram of brandy. She giggled as she handed it to me, so I surmised it was probably the dregs of many glasses. No matter—I saved it till she was gone, then I shared it with Roger. After a bit, his eyes flickered open and he was lucid. "Where are we, Bobby?" he asked. I repeated the particulars of our plight, which he had not absorbed before. Now, he seemed to understand.

"I'm frightened," he whispered. "It's so very dark."

I lit the lantern though it was not yet dusk, and I put my arm around the suffering man, lifting him so that his head rested on my shoulder. I sat against the wall supporting Roger's frail body with my arms.

"I killed a man in battle," he mourned.

His voice was so soft I had to bend my head very close to his mouth to hear him.

"I know," I said.

"I know that you know. Do not judge me." His breathing was labored. "I will thank you for that."

"I would that you, equally, will not judge me." I plunged on boldly. "I ask you to forgive me for deceiving you."

His eyes were closed and there was such a long silence, I feared he had lost consciousness, but then he murmured, "Then the night—in the fresh pool—was not a dream—Bobby?"

"Deborah. My true name is Deborah. No, it was no dream. I am no minuteman, Roger. I am a woman."

Again, he was silent. Then there was the slightest flicker of the old Roger. "Deborah? I called you Deborah once. Deborah the prophet. And you did prophesy a battle."

You remember! I thought joyfully. *Perhaps you will heal yet and all will be well.*

"Roger, I am a minutewoman, albeit against the rules of man and God. Let me tell you my story," I begged.

He did not protest, but lay against me with eyes closed as I hastily and honestly revealed to him the giveaway child, the bond servant, the teacher and spinster, and finally, the recruit, Robert Shurtliff.

"I am the unfortunate runaway bride that dim farmer was searching for on the parade ground."

Roger's face had the trace of a smile. "You are marvelous tall."

"But he lied. We were never betrothed. *Never.* He was my mother's selection for me. I donned britches and ran off to escape him."

"Yours is a strange tale," he said when I was done. Then he rested again and I feared he had slipped away, but he roused himself to seek my hand and hold it, murmuring, "A strange, sad tale, but not dishonorable."

"Thank you for that, Roger."

"You should have trusted me, Bobby, and told me at once."

"Deborah," I corrected him, weeping silently.

"I shall never know you as Deborah," he sighed. "I'll sleep now."

When he woke much later it was as if a path had been cleared for him. His breathing was fast and shallow then, as though he were racing toward some goal. "I'm only twenty-one," he panted, staring into his own private darkness. "I just began my life—barely." His body shuddered with grief.

"I wanted—one day to have a woman love me. I never had a woman. I'll never—have a child." Weak sobs racked his chest. "I'll never own my own piece of green—Concord farmland."

"A woman does love and admire you, Roger," I said softly.

But his eyes were closed and wetness glistened on his sunken cheeks. "I killed a man—in battle, Deborah," he whispered.

"He would have killed you, Roger." I tried to comfort him. "He would have sliced you like a butcher."

Roger would not hear me. "There is a stain upon my soul," he sighed.

I freed a hand to dab at the wetness on his face with a rag and then just sat quietly, my arms holding him.

About an hour later, he suddenly roused himself once more to murmur, "Thy will be done." He repeated it, sighed, and dropped his head.

His heart had stopped beating.

Weeping, I laid him flat on the dirty floor. I closed his eyes and kissed the lids.

I felt desolate.

I took some small comfort in the fact that he had recovered his senses in the end. At least, he'd put himself in the hands of God. But my faith was so badly shaken that I felt bitterness. *For whatever that's worth,* I thought. *It must be worth something. So many folks say so.* Then I was ashamed. The Congregationalists and the Baptists had abandoned me but I could not abandon my God.

For several hours I sat there in a stupor. The scent and silence of death enfolded me in that hot room. Finally I forced myself to rise and open the door. Then I moved to a place beside the window seeking any fresh air. And there I continued to sit deep in melancholy. I was roused from my lethargy by three vicious cats prowling through the open doorway. They came leaping in from another of the attic rooms and pounced on poor Roger's body. I beat them off with my musket and rolled him up in a dusty, tattered rug. I made apologies to him in my mind. *Ah, Roger. Forgive my cowardice. You deserved so much more. You deserved a better shroud. You deserved life! How I wish I could, at least, bury you in our good, clean, free earth!*

I knew that I had best make my escape quickly. I would have to leave him locked away here, for I could not carry him.

In the darkness of the night, I bolted the door of the room with his poor body in it and crept downstairs. The house was a fortress; I could not get out. All the doors were locked. I was frantic. I climbed the stairs to the first landing and tried the door next to the staircase, aware that I might be walking into a trap. It was Katharina's bedroom all right, for she heard me enter and sat up in bed.

Standing in the doorway, I whispered, "Sorry to wake you, Katharina. I must leave. My friend is dead."

"I told you not to worry about feeding him. I told you he was a dead man."

"I need you to unlock the door for me."

"Wait in the hall," she bade me, and a moment later

she emerged in a peach dressing gown. "You have time for a glass of wine before you go."

"Any moment I might be discovered," I pleaded urgently, but she led me down the stairs into the parlor and poured the wine.

I finished the filled glass in a single gulp. "I must say good-bye."

She went to the great cupboard and took from a drawer the ring of house keys.

"You must say good-bye properly." She held the keys behind her back and stood waiting, her eyes closed.

I moved silently, and with one deft reach of my arm I wrested the keys from her. "Good-bye."

"That was not gentlemanly," she started, but I had already fitted the big iron key into the front-door lock and heard it click. "I would beg a favor out of friendship. Do not report me gone to your father till the night. So I may get safely away."

"Why should I do that for you?" She pouted. "Will I ever see you again?"

"I shall surprise you," I promised.

"I will miss you." The last sound I heard was her giggle in the distance as I half limped and half ran as fast as I could manage. I was desperate to be gone, to be free of the monstrous ugliness of the Van Tassels' farmstead.

I interrupted my return journey just long enough to bathe in a mountain stream, where I splashed in the privacy of a deep thicket and used clean sand from the bottom as pumice to scrub myself. I would have to put on my filthy clothes afterward, but it didn't matter. And as I floated joyfully free, savoring the luxury of the clear, sweet water, I made a vow.

I spoke it aloud in the quiet air of the woods. "Verily, Katharina, you will be surprised!"

7. The Reckoning

Tracking toward West Point in a roundabout direction with great stealth, I made it back in several hours. A pillow was lacking so I used my haversack to rest my head as I fell into bed; nevertheless, no royal personage ever felt greater luxury than I in the confines of that small, narrow bunk surrounded by snoring Patriots. That was my first safe sleep after our dreadful ordeal.

My last thought before I closed my eyes was of poor Roger swathed in the rug. At dawn, when the drumroll of reveille roused me, I woke to his suffering face. I was haunted by his sweet ghost.

There was but one thing to do. I washed my face, tied my hair back with a cord, and, still clad in the wretched boots and dirty uniform of my captivity, hastened to see Colonel Jackson, who was in charge.

Bad luck. The colonel was not available, his aide explained; he was conferring with General Paterson, who had newly arrived. Therefore I would simply have to delay my interview and return later when he was free.

I stood undecided, not knowing what to do. An indentured servant never interrupts her master. A young woman never interrupts men in serious talk. And a private never, I was positive, interrupts officers who are conferring.

I didn't want to be presumptuous. But, remembering Roger's poor body lying on Van Tassel's floor with that foul rug for his shroud, I boldly cast off all previous bonds.

I could not wait silently! I could not brook postponement! In a loud voice, I spoke up. "I need to talk to the colonel at once!"

"Surely you can return in several hours?" The surprised aide was taken aback.

"No. You'll have to interrupt them," I replied so forcefully he was startled by my intemperate tone. "It's urgent." I struck his desk with my fist.

Staring at my scruffy, unkempt person, he seemed uncertain how to handle me. I must have looked threatening. Perhaps he thought my mind unbalanced by battle.

"Take the colonel this message," I demanded. "Private Robert Shurtliff *must* see him at once." Again I thumped the desk, this time with effective results. He scurried inside.

Whatever he told the colonel, I was immediately admitted.

"I know your name," Colonel Jackson said. "Captain Webb spoke well of you. He said you fought bravely against DeLancey's raiders and then volunteered for a dangerous mission and accomplished it. I have just commended you to General Paterson, here."

"Thank you, sir." The honor of such particular notice was both gratifying and flattering. I ducked my head, hoping neither the portly colonel nor the famous general would see my fluster.

Then I resorted to my old trick of forcing myself to cough, for I knew my very pale skin had excessively reddened. Coughing and blowing my nose and fussing, I diverted attention from my blush.

"Pardon," I said and spoke quickly once I could.

"Excuse my breaking in, but I need to report Tory activity." Briefly, I described the Van Tassel household and my own and Roger's experiences there.

"DeLancey's raiders frequent the place," I noted. "It's well situated for them to use as a hideout or stopping place. And it's handy for them as a staging ground for attacks."

"You did well to interrupt us, soldier. Can you locate the place on this map?" Colonel Jackson asked, moving over to the large wall map.

I quickly pointed to the loathsome spot.

"They're very bold, aren't they?" the colonel said. "It's right under our noses."

"We need to recover Private Snow's remains from the attic," I urged. I told them about the cats—and the heat.

"Rest your mind," the colonel assured me. "I will send a scouting party."

"Please, sir. Van Tassel tried to starve me. He allowed Private Snow to die. I request special permission to go on this raid. I know the premises and the enemy. And I have plenty of personal reasons."

"But, soldier. Look at you. You've been through an ordeal. You've a terrible cough. What you need is plenty of rest, so you can recover."

I had coughed myself right into trouble. "Please, sir, Roger Snow died in my arms."

General Paterson, who had been listening in silence, intervened now. "Let the soldier go. He has earned the right. In fact, I'd put him in charge of the search party."

"Yes, sir. Shurtliff, take whoever you need and whatever you need. I leave this matter in your capable hands."

"Thank you, sir."

Twenty volunteers readily stepped forward to join me in the scouting and burial party. Quickly, we made ready, setting out by twos in the late afternoon. Once close, we hid in the woods near Van Tassel's place to wait for the arrival of any Tory visitors.

I watched from the cover of the woods and felt curiously patient. Waiting merely sharpened my appetite for taking out this vicious nest of vipers and particularly the worst viper of them all, Van Tassel. I, who had never really lusted to kill anybody, not even during battle, and had thought it was my womanliness that restrained me, now recognized coolly that I could readily kill Van Tassel. It wouldn't come to that, but if it did . . .

Darkness fell at last and brought with it sporadic visitors over the next few hours, in twos and threes, altogether a total of nineteen Tories. Swaggerers and louts on magnificent horses probably stolen, they appeared a mighty tempting quarry to us concealed Patriots. Every time the front door closed after newcomers, some eager scout behind a tree whispered, "Ready now?"

"Not yet," I cautioned. "Wait. It's better to let them get good and drunk. We'll give them till midnight. By then even their guards will be rolling drunk."

The sounds of revelry grew louder and more violent during the passing hours. At midnight, on signal, we first opened the stables and emptied them of horses; then we burst into Van Tassel's house, muskets at the ready.

The befuddled Tories were truly astonished, so much so that one mustached, burly brute dressed up like a peacock immediately vomited all over his brocade waistcoat. Several captives surprisingly let flow unmanly, drunken tears. Brave Tories weeping? A pretty sight!

"You are all prisoners of war. Surrender your arms or you are dead," I ordered.

"You?" Van Tassel exclaimed on catching sight of me.

"Yes," I said agreeably. "Me."

He looked dazed. The shift in power was too swift for him.

"Remember when you took us in, you said hospitality here was limited in wartime? You could find no bed for a sick man?" I looked around at the abundance of drinks and meats and pastries. "It does look like you're running an inn for Tories here."

Suddenly, I just wanted to have done with him. "Traitor," I accused. "We will empty your storerooms and cellar of the loot from Patriot farms. You will be allowed to remain in the house for now, but you'll be arrested and hanged if you ever again host Tories."

Van Tassel opened and closed his mouth soundlessly like a bloated fish. I chose to take no notice and went on speaking. "Just remember that a Continental soldier died in your home—died at your hands," I charged more accurately.

"No." The Dutchman was panicked. "He came here sick. That was not my fault."

Just then, who should come flouncing out of the never-locked bedroom but Katharina herself. She tripped quickly down the steps, eager to return to the party. Elegantly appareled in an emerald green gown with large bows shelving and emphasizing her ample bosom, she had her hair up and curled, a jewel at her neck.

When she saw the soldiers—and then me, musket in hand—she stopped short.

"Katharina, me darlin', come give me a hand," whined the drunkard who'd messed his clothing. He was dabbing at himself with a linen napkin.

"You'd best go back to your room," I instructed her. "The party's over."

Staring, unbelieving, she continued down the stairs and stopped in front of me. She pointed her finger. "*I* brought him food," she said smugly to the assemblage, as if she'd been my great benefactor. She looked about vainly for an officer in charge. Seeing none, she spoke to me haughtily. "Tell the others. You must speak for me."

My lips remained sealed.

Now smiling winsomely at my companions in arms, she confided, "I was Bobby Shurtliff's friend. Ask him."

"She did bring food," I acknowledged, "leavings from the floor with dust balls that she didn't bother to brush off. But she was never a friend."

My eyes fixed on her feet, and I remembered the shoes. She'd chosen the wrong pair if she wanted my sympathy. "I recognize the toe of that slipper," I said. "It prodded my poor dying friend." I raised my leg and poked in imitation of her cruelty. "You Tories do not understand friendship. You burn your neighbors' houses and steal their horses and their goods.

"Miss, you'd best go back upstairs," I dismissed her. "You have no place down here."

"How dare you?" She glared at me. "Where is the officer in command?"

"I am in command here, now."

"You are no officer."

"Ours is a citizens' army. Even privates may command."

Outrage made her falter. "You—you!" she sputtered. "You've betrayed me."

"No. I kept my word and surprised you just as I promised. Now, you're in the way."

I took a step forward so that she had to back up. Again I stepped forward, relentlessly. "Upstairs. We've no time for you. Unless you'd like to help clean up your smelly friend." I pointed to the Tory who'd called after her.

Her face reddened and distorted with rage, she gathered her skirts and began to ascend the stairs.

"Katharina . . . ," the messy fellow lamented, but she just kept going.

With no bloodshed, we returned to West Point bringing nineteen prisoners and nine captured horses—as well as a hoard of food stores, cured meats, grain, and wine. A volunteer and I took charge of Roger's body. It was pitifully light.

We held a simple burial service at sunset. The hovering clouds effaced the waning light quickly and heightened the bleakness of the occasion. I stood at attention and tried to heed the ancient words of the Twenty-third Psalm, which Jennie and I had memorized and recited so long ago when she first learned to read—comforting words now repeated for Private Roger Snow, who walked through the valley of the shadow of death. The reading was followed by the slow, piercing notes of the bugle calling farewell.

All through that day I thought about Van Tassel and the raid and the burial. The only relief in my mind's eye, for a moment, was the perverse, pleasurable memory of a furious Katharina holding her elegant skirts as she fled up the stairs. Life would be boring for her now because the house would be carefully watched. There wouldn't be much company—we'd see to it.

Katharina might even have to read a book for entertainment. She could benefit from some of Ben Franklin's good advice: *Experience keeps a dear school, but fools will learn in no other.*

I was glad I hadn't had to shoot Van Tassel. He was rotten and I did not want his taint. Though war had changed and hardened me, my love for Roger had tempered my spirit, and at the core of the Robert Shurtliff in charge of the Van Tassel house detail, I'd recognized the woman Deborah Sampson. I remained myself.

During evening parade, Colonel Jackson called out, "Private Shurtliff, front and center."

It was never good to be singled out. I stepped forth nervously.

"I wish to honor the success of the raid on the Tory Van Tassel's house." He presented me then with a large bottle of fine wine. "Treat your men," he advised. "They've earned it."

My response surprised him and, in fact, I surprised myself. "Sir, may I have one more bottle?"

"Eh?" The colonel was taken aback by my apparent greediness.

"One more bottle so that the prisoners might fare in a like manner."

"What? Would you treat men who want only to destroy us?"

"They're people—like us. Please, sir, I'd like to do it in honor of Private Snow, who believed we can't teach anyone virtue unless they see it in us. He didn't want to injure anyone or starve anyone—not even our enemies. I agree with him. I don't want to be like Van Tassel."

The colonel handed over a second jug of wine, and I took it to the prisoners. I unloosened the wrists of the prisoner nearest me—the mustached Tory thug now unadorned by his spoiled brocade waistcoat—and gave him the bottle. He drank greedily, but when I began to retie his wrists he suddenly reached out and hit me and knocked me to the ground. I rose quickly to make a second try, and he struck once more. This time I warded off the blow.

"What's wrong with ye? The lad has got a good heart. He's come to wet our whistles. Leave off," the other Tory prisoners jeered at him, but he cursed me. "Damn you. You stole my wench and then you took me prisoner. Damn you to hell."

"Stole your wench?" I was bewildered. "Not I." I'd never seen the man before the capture and knew nothing of what he was saying.

Now I was not bewildered but thoroughly disgusted to be thought the rival of this brute. What sort of misguided tale had he been told? "You are mistaken," I protested.

"Don't give me that. Katharina was in love with you. She'd no time for me. She could only think about the baby-faced rebel." Furious, he tried to rush me again, but this time he was seized and tied up by guards.

Fifty lashes were delivered to his naked back; then he went on trial with the others and was imprisoned in Fishkill.

I relived those terrible attic weeks constantly in my mind. I faulted myself. So many reproaches, so many things I should have done: Yes, I should have spoken, I should have found a way to tell Roger how fond of him I was, how much I admired his honesty and his gentleness. Why hadn't I told him the truth sooner?

Because I saw myself as a lesser creature, a mere female whose deception somehow made her unworthy and would offend him. How stupid! Captain Simeon Sampson, my father's cousin, had earned honor for his woman's disguise. Paul Revere and John Hancock had dumped the tea in Boston harbor camouflaged in Indian paint and feathers.

Yet, when the man I loved lay dying I failed him, fearing to reveal my true self. I was too weak to cast off my disguise. If ever I had a chance to redeem myself as a woman, I would do it, I vowed. I would, no matter the risk.

Often in my free hours, I would wander back to the small cemetery to sit beside the new grave and talk to Roger, just as I had in the attic when I knew he probably couldn't hear. But he *had* heard then, and perhaps somewhere, somehow, he could hear now.

"I miss you, Roger. I've had enough of war. My clothes are rags, my shoes torn. I have a gimpy leg, so I'll never walk quite right again. The army is in disarray. The Continental Congress has no money to pay us. If only they'd finish making the peace. . . ."

I'd clear up the few fallen twigs and leaves around his grave while I talked to him. "You did no wrong, Roger. The Tory you killed would have killed you. He had already done you great harm. You were bleeding badly and he had his saber ready. You had no choice. That's what war means: no choice.

"And, Roger—a woman did love and admire you. I doubt you heard me tell you this but it is so. I, Deborah Sampson, loved you. True, I have an odd mind for a woman. Deacon Thomas told me so many times, but I am just an ordinary woman who had an unusual idea. I believed I could serve my country just as a man does. Thus I had to do it concealed."

I had not wept publicly in all the time I'd been in the army. In order to survive, just as I could not drink water for my thirst or answer nature's calls normally, I dared not cry. Such luxury of feeling was only for women.

But sitting beside Roger's bare, sandy grave, I gave way. The cemetery was isolated and no others came to mourn for these lonely dead buried so far from their homes and kin. My sobs were for Roger and for myself, and for all those others lost in this long, long war.

When I emerged, dry-eyed and straight-shouldered, manly in appearance, I was Robert Shurtliff once again.

Not long after our interview, Colonel Jackson sent for me. "General Paterson's aide is not well," the colonel informed me, "and the general would like you to replace him. You impressed the general. He thought you seemed a conscientious and sensible soldier. If you take the job, you will assist him personally as well as his staff officers, and live in their compound. It is an honor to be chosen, Shurtliff."

I would live in their compound instead of being cooped up with five other men in the tiny, windowless space where I could not escape the constant drinking, gambling, and cursing.

Had I not the training? Had I not been a bond servant for ten years? General Paterson must have sensed that I was peculiarly suited to the assignment. Did I want to be the general's "waiter"?

I'd thought I was done with serving when I became a masterless woman at eighteen.

Ah, but there was a great difference this time. I *liked* the peacetime army! And I *admired* General Paterson. He was a war hero, a wise, smart, handsome commander whose men respected him.

Nobody could sign me over; I was my own person. This was my decision and I could choose. I did not hesitate long. General Paterson would never appoint himself *in loco parentis.* Even though, in a way, he was: He was father to his men. I liked that, for I'd gone so long without a father and he was an admirable man.

"I accept, sir."

I would serve the general with all my heart, and perhaps if my secret was ever revealed, General Paterson might deal gently with me. Surely he could not sentence me to death if I served him faithfully.

What a pleasure it was to move into better quarters and live among the officers, though they drank and gambled and cursed and whored just like the enlisted men—maybe even more so, for the officers had more money and freedom and luxury than the common recruits. I concluded that these flaws were in the characters of most men.

I, who never cursed or used foul language, who was Christian and chaste, had to deflect attention from myself, and I did my best to be agreeable, helpful, and, on rowdy occasions, invisible.

For three months I waited on the general at table, took care of his uniforms, and sometimes was his secretary or his courier, running errands for both him and his wife. I was given a fine stallion to ride.

A brilliant military man, General Paterson, who had been a lawyer before the war, was kind and civil. He even liked a joke with his men now and then. When I completed a mission and served him well, he was generous with his compliments, which made me feel happy and safe. I needed to be a good soldier to be above suspicion, and I worked diligently at it.

✻ ✻ ✻

Then, in the summer of 1783, it all changed. The general received sudden orders to proceed to troubled Philadelphia to lead fifteen hundred troops. Rebellious Patriots—Pennsylvania soldiers, on hearing that they were to be discharged without receiving their back pay—were threatening mutiny. His task would be to quell any disturbance.

I was to follow several days afterward with most of the general's goods.

All around me, men were leaving, going home. It was a temptation to decamp.

The newspapers had been writing about the seething rebellion for weeks. The problem was that the Continental Congress had no money for soldiers' wages. Only the states had the right to raise the needed money through taxes, and the states were hesitant. The desperate, unpaid mutineers had besieged the Congress.

What was I to think?

These mutineers were men who'd fought on my side and together we'd won the war. None of us was being paid. We were all poor, ragged, and disappointed, and only for those reasons were these veterans threatening our new government. They were not bad men. In a way, they were me. Yet, they were not me.

I had to sort out my loyalties.

General Paterson had been good to me. And I had my orders. I was in the army and army men obey rules. Our commander in chief, General Washington, had bade the discharged men to return home, pay or no pay. I understood their disappointment.

But orders are orders.

And that was what I finally decided they ought to do: obey General Washington's orders. Go home without their money.

Home? In truth, I had no home to go to. Mother certainly would not honor my military service. She would not welcome me; she would feel I'd disgraced her. My church would not have me. The Leonards would not employ me to weave and spin, nor would any other respectable family in Middleborough. Teaching school was now an impossibility.

I would be a pariah, an outcast.

At least in Philadelphia, work with General Paterson would offer safety—and adventure.

Had I not, years before, confided to Jennie that seeing the City of Brotherly Love was one of my girlhood dreams? Now I set out with high hopes. Was it at last possible that I would really get to see the capital of the United States?

A frenzy of excitement built up within me as I journeyed, only to crumble on all sides when I arrived in Philadelphia.

The city was in great distress.

For months it had been devastated by smallpox and measles and, more recently, yellow fever. The streets echoed with the rumble of the wheels of the heavy carts overloaded with the sick and the dead. The mournful bells warned pedestrians away.

Troops were quarantined outside the city as a precaution because soldiers like me, who'd had little contact with these diseases, were particularly vulnerable.

I arrived to find that General Paterson's previous aide had returned to his old job. There was no longer a need for me.

"Thank you for your loyalty and service." The general was most kind. "You will rejoin your company camped outside the city. I trust you may yet have a chance to see our beautiful Philadelphia, the cradle of the new nation."

Shortly thereafter I fell ill. Of course, I resisted medical attention and attempted to treat myself, but then I became so sick I lost consciousness. Before a fort-night had passed, Mike, the plague-cart driver, was sum-moned and delivered me to the hospital and Dr. Binney.

Mindful of the passing time in Dr. Binney's care and the need to complete my story, I dedicated my strength and waking hours to writing, neatly but quickly. I wasted no time particularly after Dr. Binney, in the third week of my stay, instructed me to practice getting off the bed and slowly walking about the room, with a cane at first and then by grasping on to furniture or shelves. I dressed in full uniform, slowly; stayed dressed for several hours, writing seated in a chair; then returned to bed each day. Initially, these slight efforts at normal living exhausted me, but I could feel myself getting stronger and steadier.

My voice was not fully returned. Of late, each time the doctor visited he greeted me, "Good evening, Private Shurtliff," and I attempted to answer, aloud, "Good evening, Dr. Binney." My whispers now could be readily heard, but I was not eager to waste time talking. I wanted to write, and several nights in the last week of my allot-ted month I wrote by lamplight till quite late. I knew the doctor would kindly extend my time there if needed, but

I did not want that to happen. Yearning to accomplish what I had pledged to do, I was desperately eager to know my fate, whatever it might be.

I was sitting up in bed on the day I'd finished writing, ready and waiting when he came, and in my hand I held the little silver desk key.

I offered it to him immediately. "Here, sir," I said—and those words were clearly spoken, as if a miracle had occurred—my own voice had its true tone.

"Ah, one voice replaces the other." He was delighted. "You have done with the written voice—for now." He rubbed his hands in anticipation.

He had never once hurried me or troubled me, but had tended my medical needs all these weeks, with his servants helping and his good wife supervising the kitchen below. He was a monument to patience and discretion. I owed this man my life.

"Your voice will grow stronger, but slowly, slowly, all in good time. You are practically fully recovered.

"Tomorrow and the next couple of days, you may celebrate by getting up in the mornings and staying up all day, Private Shurtliff. In your uniform, of course. The masquerade must continue till you are gone from here. I have brought several books for you, including a copy of *A Thousand and One Nights*, so you can reread an old friend, if you like, while I peruse your manuscript." He handed me the books, and then he proceeded to unlock the desk drawer and remove the substantial stack of paper. "No other eyes than mine shall see this," he promised once again. "You have my word."

He went off then with all my secrets.

I suffered agonies imagining him reading my text, a man privy to a young woman's most personal thoughts and secrets. But I comforted myself: *He is a doctor. He rescued me. He would never do me harm or think ill of me.*

He appeared three nights later and was most respectful.

"Private Shurtliff, you have given an extraordinary account of yourself. I am honored that you trusted me sufficiently to confide so thoroughly in me. There is much to be learned from your story."

"Thank you, sir. Some of it was not easy to admit to."

"I cannot imagine any scribe who could have done it better."

I have stored that word *scribe* in the strongbox of my heart, along with *Yankee rose* from Father, *Deborah Smart* from Cousin Ruth, and *keen* from the Thomases' tutor. These are the jewels that no one can ever steal from me.

"I am returning your pages to you." He had put them in a handsome, burnished leather case, which he now handed me. "You have written so well that I wish to suggest a brave untrodden path for you. Your story should be published—"

"Oh no!" I interrupted.

"—Published that the world might know of human capacities, women's capacities, of bravery and courage and love of country. That would be a tribute to your Roger Snow. I think it would make him very proud. Do not decide now. Think about it, consider it.

"Tomorrow morning, I shall discharge you, fully cured, and send you packing. Be up and ready early, soldier."

Nancy Bailey, her bodice ripped open running the gauntlet in Elizabethtown, came into my head that night as I stared at the leather case that held my story and wondered at my fate. I had no doubt but that I would be delivered to the army authorities in the morning. Probably the doctor would take me by carriage to a military post and turn me in. Surely he would not want his wife and daughters involved in a disagreeable scene of arrest here. And then . . . ?

My mind refused to go further. It was too terrible to contemplate.

I had not long to wait. Dr. Binney appeared early, a letter in his hand, his seal set heavily in wax in three places upon the envelope.

"I have written a letter to General John Paterson at West Point. I know you are without pocket money, so here is a small sum for your immediate needs. A man should not travel without some pence in his pocket." He passed me a handful of pounds and shillings.

"I shall return it, sir."

He shrugged. "It is of no matter."

"Doctor, will you answer me one question?"

"If I can."

"Why were you so good to me? Why did you go to such trouble?"

The question seemed to truly surprise him. "I am part of a noble profession," he said. "I took the Hippocratic oath promising to preserve and value human life. Your predicament was dire. You would have died in hospital."

"Thank you," I said.

"And now, Private Shurtliff, it would please me very much to shake your hand."

I thrust forth my hand, and the good doctor shook it as vigorously as if I were another man, then he suddenly reached out to embrace me heartily as a brother.

"You are a brave soldier, Private Shurtliff," he said, his voice husky.

"Thank you again for my life, sir," I replied.

"You more than earned it in the service of your country."

"Even though I am . . . ?" I could not help but ask.

"Most particularly *because* you are."

His wife and two young daughters stood on the gallery and waved gaily, probably relieved at last at the departure of the strange, mute invalid who had taken so much of the doctor's time.

I waved to them. I had left a grateful note for Mrs. Binney, whose kindnesses had been daily evident in the fine food and drink and the lovely blossoms on the food trays.

The doctor opened the coach door and bade me enter. Then he shut the door, remaining outside on the cobblestone walk.

What? Was he not coming along to deliver me with his letter?

Reaching up, he handed me the thick envelope through the opened window. "Private Shurtliff, you will present this letter in person to General John Paterson." Turning to the coachman, he ordered, "Take Private

Shurtliff to West Point—unless he has some prior desti-
nation, which he may tell you himself."

I could not believe my ears. He was sending me
alone, unsupervised? Was I being tested or perhaps, was
it possible, just trusted? Dr. Binney was as much a mystery as he had been all along.

"Good luck!" he called, moving away up the walk.
"Godspeed."

The coachman set off.

For the first dozen miles or so, I sat hunched up as if
I'd been chained to the seat. I was thoroughly enmeshed
in the dilemma Dr. Binney had created and unable to
free myself. Only once, when I heard the tolling of the
bell on a plague cart, did I rouse myself to look out. I
recognized Mike's ruddy face and saw the wretched pile
of bodies passing close, and I realized again how much I
owed my savior.

My eyes fixed on the letter in my hand. A loyal army
doctor, Dr. Binney surely had reported my bizarre and
illegal situation truthfully. The penalties for such trans-
gressions were severe and well known: the lash, the
gauntlet, or prison. Perhaps the doctor had pleaded for
leniency for me.

Again, my mind turned to Nancy Bailey and other young women caught in the same crime I had committed. I trembled.

Unspeakable disgrace would be heaped upon me, a young woman of good Pilgrim stock descended from Miles Standish, John and Priscilla Alden, and Governor Bradford of Plymouth Colony. The name Sampson would be filth on people's lips.

I could stop the coach on a deserted road somewhere outside the city and burn the damaging letter and all my handwritten pages as well. Then I could disappear to emerge in some far place, unknown, another person—I could flee. I could vanish as my beloved father had, so long ago.

No—in truth, after those first wild and desperate minutes of my carriage ride, I could not and would not contemplate that.

It was an unworthy, demeaning idea. I cast it from me at once like some sullied shawl.

I was weary of being someone else and living someone else's life. The doctor had given me a clear choice: honesty or deception. In doing that, he had expressed his faith in me, in my character, which he now knew better than any other human. The integrity of Deborah Sampson was real to him even though he knew only Robert Shurtliff.

I would affirm that faith.

"West Point straight on?" the driver inquired.

"West Point," I agreed, forever closing my mind to escape. "Straight on."

And so, after a long and tiring journey, the coachman bade me good luck and left me on the familiar parade grounds. *I am home at last,* I thought gratefully. *This is where I truly belong.*

"Well, I'll be damned! A ghost!" the first of my tent-mates who got a glimpse of me shouted, bringing the others tumbling outside. They'd all been positive I had died of the malignant fever and they now assured me cheerfully that they'd burned candles for me.

How noisily they welcomed me back and rejoiced in my rebirth!

If you knew I was Deborah Sampson, a woman, would you still be glad? I wondered. *We shall see, for soon you will know. And when I am whipped and reviled, and the mob rails at you for being my tentmates and never discovering me, will you defend me? I fear not.*

"No one reads us the news like you, Bobby, with feelin'." One comrade who could not read had sorely missed me. A loud, jolly argument started over who deserved the credit for shipping me off with Mike in his plague cart. "You owe us drinks. We saved your life, boy," they teased.

"You just wanted more room in the tent. You thought you were rid of me, but I fooled you." I put them off good-naturedly. Though it was wonderful to be back, I was pressed to do what I had been charged to.

Once I had freshened up, I took the damning letter in hand and set out for the reckoning. There was no point postponing it: What must come must come.

With enormous misgivings and pitiful small courage I headed for the general's office.

General Paterson was writing at his desk, and, once he saw it was me, he rose rapidly to come round and welcome me. "Private Shurtliff, we thought you were dead. We were so sorry."

"I was very ill, sir. I have a letter here from Dr. Binney in Philadelphia that describes the particulars." I handed it over.

"Dr. Binney? I know the man. He once took one of my men from a pile of dead bodies. A saber had ripped the fellow open and his bowels were hanging out—but he was still alive. Binney tucked the bowels in, sewed him up, and he recovered. Remarkable surgeon. Remarkable.

"At ease, Private, while I read his letter." He returned to his chair and sliced the flap open.

Leaning back, he began to study it. As he continued, he straightened up in his chair and his countenance altered dramatically. With surprise and doubt and baffled laughter, at first, the general absorbed Dr. Binney's words. He raised his eyes to look at me, then looked down, then looked up again. "Shurtliff, this is surely some sort of ill-advised and monstrous prank?"

"No, sir."

"Then you are telling me that *that* military uniform conceals a female form?"

"Yes, sir."

He signaled—elbow on his desk and palm raised— that I should say no more while he read on. The letter filled three long vellum sheets, and he paid close attention to every word. Then he studied all of it over again before he finally put it down.

He shook his head vigorously, as if he'd had a blow to the skull and had to rouse himself, then he rose and came close, walking around me slowly, inspecting me. "Take your hat off," he ordered, "and loosen your hair."

I did as I was told.

"Impossible!" he said. "Absolutely impossible! I could not have a woman living so close and serving me thus and not know it."

"Sir, I am a woman."

"Truly?"

"On my honor, sir." My voice faltered. I was shaking uncontrollably. "I hope I shall not have to die"—my voice broke—"for my deception, sir?"

He stood there silent, deep in thought, not responding to my frightened words.

"I ask you for mercy, General Paterson."

"How did you get back here, Shurtliff?"

"The doctor put me in a coach."

"You came alone?"

"Yes, sir."

"Why did you not flee?"

I hesitated. "I was charged to deliver the letter, sir."

"Come now, Shurtliff, again I ask you, why did you not flee? You were free to go your way. To take the letter and just cut and run like so many others are doing."

"I did not flee because the doctor trusted me." I stopped and corrected myself. I would not be dishonest now. "No, that's true, but it is not the whole truth. I didn't cut and run because—I'd always hoped for an honorable discharge."

There, I had said it now in all its boldness and impossibility.

"But you're a woman."

"I know, sir."

He sat down at his desk once more and reread the letter. "Shurtliff, who else knows about this?"

"Only the doctor, you, and I, sir."

"Well—I believe Colonel Jackson, who thinks so highly of you, ought to be informed." His tone was, oddly, not angry. There even seemed to be a peculiar mischievous glint in his eyes.

So, at least he was not enraged or revolted by the idea of a woman in uniform. My spirits were a little lifted by this unexpected turn.

He stood directly in front of me and studied me. "I would like to test the good colonel. He is dining here with me in an hour. Could you make yourself over into your other self?" He glanced at the letter. "Could you be Deborah Sampson tonight if I supplied the means?"

"Yes, sir."

"Very well. My wife is away visiting her family but her wardrobe is largely in our rooms in the family quarters. Choose what garments you need and dress there. I shall see that you're not disturbed." He stopped speaking to plan for a moment. "When I send for you, you will be the young lady Deborah Sampson, and you will give no clue to what has transpired."

I didn't know what to think, but I had little time to worry about it. I had to get ready but first choose the costume quickly. Mistress Paterson's wardrobe was vast and costly—I'd never seen so many lovely frocks.

I chose a white linen costume trimmed with Belgian ivory lace at the sleeves and the hem, and white boots that were quite suitable. The garments were beautifully made. Katharina Van Tassel would have killed for such delicate lace trimming. The boots pinched a bit on the sides, but, fortunately, the general's wife had quite large feet. I had to quickly take in the skirt at the waist because its width was for a woman of more than ample girth. The blouse would do fine just tucked in.

I also needed time to rehearse being feminine. Dainty gestures were never first habit for me, but after so long living among men and aping their rough ways, I needed retraining in basic womanhood. I could still curtsey, I found, and that cheered me until I thought of Nancy Bailey and what curtseying had done for her.

With alacrity, I removed the tight chest-binder that I'd fashioned so long ago. It was truly a pleasure to have breasts again, to not have to deny part of my body. And the softness of the lady's fine garments caressed my skin. I could not resist the beguiling scent of roses in a gorgeous cut-glass container. I dabbed it lavishly behind my earlobes.

I was ready when the fist sounded the death knell at the door. "Colonel Jackson is here and I am eager to introduce you, Miss Sampson."

Walking carefully in unaccustomed narrow boots, I made my way into the room where the two men were sitting on large chairs drinking wine.

They rose.

General Paterson blinked hard at the transformation of Robert Shurtliff. "Miss Sampson," he murmured and took a sizable sip from his glass.

I curtseyed, but bounced up in recovery too quickly, I feared.

He needed another draught of wine before he could

manage his introductions. "Colonel Jackson, I should like to present my charming guest, Miss Deborah Sampson. She is from your own state, Massachusetts. Miss Sampson, this is Colonel Henry Jackson."

"Delighted." The colonel bowed.

Again, I curtseyed. I moved much more slowly than before, trying for grace. It was, therefore, a long curtsey.

"She is visiting briefly, but I wanted very much for you to meet her. I felt it imperative."

"I'm charmed," said Colonel Jackson, who was surely wondering why it was imperative but was too much the gentleman to inquire.

"Miss Sampson is related to someone you know well," General Paterson went on. "I wonder if you can see the resemblance."

The colonel studied me with new interest.

"In fact, you have actually met Miss Sampson herself before."

It was plain to see that General Paterson was having difficulty maintaining his decorous demeanor. He was a man who laughed easily and the colonel's puzzlement was amusing.

Colonel Jackson, after a careful study of my appearance, gave up, totally mystified. "I don't know any

Sampsons," he said by way of polite excuse. "You are surely mistaken, John."

"Scrutinize her face well," the general urged, laughing outright now. To me he said, "Please indulge me and do not think this request rude, but walk about the room a little so that he might see you in motion and, perhaps, recognize a familiar gait?"

I walked as daintily and elegantly as someone else's pinching boots might allow.

"No," the baffled colonel said. "No." He laughed apologetically. "Sorry. You ring no bell."

"Very well," the general said. "Miss Sampson is the lady's true name and you do, actually, know *her*—you know this very same person by a pseudonym."

"Impossible!" Colonel Jackson objected.

"The very word *I* used when she first confronted me!" the general exclaimed. "But you do know her, Henry."

"I do?" Now Colonel Jackson was astonished. "Who are you, ma'am?" he demanded of me.

I rose and saluted. "I am Private Robert Shurtliff, sir. Fourth Massachusetts Regiment. Light Rangers."

"Impossible!" he said again and sat down abruptly. "Absolutely impossible!"

"Thank you, Shurtliff. Now go and dress, and be liberal with the soap and water. You smell like a rose-bush. Meanwhile, I shall give Henry here some further stimulant and allow him to read Dr. Binney's letter."

Gladly, I hurried off to change my clothes, relieved to be out of the presence of these two officers I had successfully deceived for so long.

They had been mightily intrigued by the novelty of my reappearance. Once that was over, there would be reflection and judgment and then a meting out of justice for my crime. *Only let it not be death or public disgrace,* I prayed over and over as I carefully pulled the basting stitches from the skirt and hung the white outfit neatly in the closet. I scrubbed my skin vigorously, but could not rid myself of the rose scent. I was, indeed, a walking nosegay.

"You may sit," the general invited when I returned.

The colonel kept staring at me. "Excuse me," he said, "you make an attractive woman—and a dashing soldier. It will take a little while for me to get used to both of you."

"I'm sorry," I began, "to give you this trouble. . . ."

Instead of responding, he then began to laugh helplessly and the general, equally amused, joined him.

My mumbled apologies and pleas went unheard. Novelty still reigned.

I waited till all was quiet to plead my case again. "Sirs, I know the punishment for dissembling is severe. . . ."

The general was wiping tears of merriment from his eyes. "Do not think we were laughing at you. We were laughing at ourselves because you, a young woman, outfoxed us both."

"Sir, I wanted only to serve my country."

Now he addressed the issue seriously. "Private Shurtliff, you seem to have served it honorably. Dr. Binney looked into the records and his extraordinary letter attests to that. He calls you a heroine and a brave fighter, and says you volunteered for dangerous missions and were wounded in action.

"I, too, shall check your records, of course, but I believe that just as your service with me was excellent, so must your entire record be. I consider myself a good judge of men."

"And women too, I suppose," the colonel ragged him.

"Yes, and especially of one particular woman. For the time being, Private Shurtliff, we will use your services here at headquarters until we determine what's to be done with you. Say nothing of any of this and report to me in the morning. Eat some garlic to get rid of that scent."

"Then I will be neither whipped nor jailed, sir?"

"For serving your country loyally and fighting bravely? I daresay you need not fear such fierce punishment. The war is almost at its end; permanent peace is at hand. It's merely a matter of weeks now. I cannot promise you more presently. You must let time work out its pattern."

I thanked God that I had come so incredibly far unscathed.

I contented myself for the next two months working on General Paterson's staff. Never by any word or gesture was my peculiar identity alluded to. I did my tasks energetically and efficiently and the general was often pleased with me. He said so.

Sometimes Colonel Jackson came on army business, and he was brisk and very military in his manner. Only once, when we were alone in the general's office, where on the desk stood a vase of roses, did the visiting colonel wink at me. I did not wink back, but I appreciated how lucky I had been in my friends.

On September 3, 1783, we had peace.

On October 25, 1783, Private Robert Shurtliff was awarded an honorable discharge from the army at West Point. General Henry Knox, the officer in command, signed it. Colonel Henry Jackson and General John Paterson filed certificates attesting to Shurtliff's bravery and loyalty.

Honorably discharged has not yet joined *scribe, keen, Deborah Smart,* and *Yankee rose.* Those were honors awarded directly to Deborah Sampson.

My biggest consideration was the charge Dr. Binney put to me. It was a frightening idea, and I could not decide. Then one morning I woke, and, just as years before I knew I had to leave my church and become a Baptist, so now I knew I had to publish this manuscript, if some printer would agree.

The book will forever honor Roger Snow.

It is my dream that my true service to my country will then be recognized as a woman's effort.

I know there will be scorn and calumny for the

"woman soldier," but I live in hope that there may also be, one day, perhaps, an honorable discharge for Deborah Sampson, Minutewoman, which I can store in the strongbox of my heart.

Then I will no longer be a solitary rider.

Author's Note

Deborah Sampson is truly a dream heroine—but she was real.

I first heard of her about five years ago when I was visiting my family in Cambridge, Massachusetts, and Anatol, my young grandson, showed me a picture book with sketches of a maiden in the uniform of a Continental army soldier. "She was very brave," he assured me earnestly.

Indeed, she was brave. Born in the Massachusetts Bay Colony in 1760 and abandoned by her father at five, Deborah was a "give-away child." At the age of eight, she was indentured as a farm servant and bonded for ten years, during which she managed to educate herself. She loved to read and had a great curiosity about the world.

Once she was a "masterless" woman, she earned her living as a schoolteacher as well as a spinster and weaver.

These were the tumultuous years of the American Revolution and Deborah was intensely patriotic, though it was a time when women were not supposed to be involved in politics.

But Deborah dreamed a prophetic dream three times, in which destiny summoned her. Her poignant recollection of that dream first appeared in her 1797 autobiography, *The Female Review: or, Memoirs of an American Young Lady,* edited by Herman Mann.

Tall and very strong from her years of hard labor, she disguised herself as a man and enlisted for three years in the Continental army, serving heroically—she was twice gravely wounded and had to treat herself so that her secret would not be discovered. She successfully extracted a musket ball from her own thigh without anesthetic.

The rest of her army career was even more incredible. She was found out only when she lost consciousness from a fever and an army doctor sought to feel her heartbeat. For some reason, the doctor continued to keep her secret, and with his wife's assistance nursed Deborah back to health.

All that I have mentioned thus far is amply documented,

but Deborah's army years and what happened to her afterward have become legends, so nobody knows exactly what is fact. The very spelling of her family name and of her alias are disputed.

I tried to tell her story as accurately as I could, imagining what I didn't know. Therefore, while the biographical details are indeed factual, the dialogue, the romance with Roger Snow, and some characters, including coquettish Katharina, are my invention.

An honorable discharge from the United States Army was issued to Deborah Sampson (under her assumed name, Robert Shurtliff) in 1783. She could not return to Plympton, her mother's village, after her army escapade—even with the honorable discharge—so she went to Sharon, a nearby village, and there met and married a local farmer, Benjamin Gannett, with whom she had three children. When the family came upon hard times, Deborah once again donned the blue and white uniform to become the first woman lecturer in the United States. Musket in hand, she appeared in theaters as the opening act before a play, and she would then perform twenty-seven military gun drills before speaking of her experiences and apologizing for having worn "britches."

She received an army pension after Paul Revere wrote a letter on her behalf, and in 1827 she died at the age of sixty-six.

On May 23, 1983, Governor Michael S. Dukakis signed a proclamation honoring Deborah Sampson as the "Official Heroine of the Commonwealth of Massachusetts." She was the first person in the United States—hero or heroine—to be so honored by a state.

Chronology

December 17, 1760   Deborah Sampson, a descendant of Miles Standish and John and Priscilla Alden, is born in Plympton, Massachusetts Bay Colony.

1765   Deborah Sampson's father mysteriously disappears.

1768   Deborah Sampson becomes an indentured servant till she is eighteen.

December 16, 1773   The date of the Boston Tea Party, when American Patriots dumped tea in Boston harbor to protest unfair British taxation; also the eve of Deborah Sampson's thirteenth birthday.

April 18, 1775   Paul Revere rides by night to warn Patriots that the British are coming to attack.

April 19, 1775   The Battle of Lexington and Concord, the first battle of the Revolutionary War, is waged.

1776   Thomas Paine's *Common Sense,* calling for rebellion, is circulated and avidly read by citizens, including Deborah Sampson.

1778   Deborah Sampson finishes her indenture and is a masterless woman.

October 19, 1781   Cornwallis and the British surrender at Yorktown after six years of bitter fighting, but there is no formal peace; vicious guerrilla warfare continues.

May 20, 1782   Robert Shurtliff enlists in Bellingham, Massachusetts Bay Colony.

July 16, 1782   Deborah Sampson writes a letter to her mother telling her she is employed in a large and respectable household and that her employers are disciplinarians.

Summer 1782   Robert Shurtliff is wounded twice in the guerrilla warfare with recalcitrant Tories. He survives and thrives in the army.

Summer 1783   Robert Shurtliff contracts a "malignant fever" in the Philadelphia epidemic and nearly dies.

September 3, 1783   The formal end of the Revolutionary War, at last: The Treaty of Paris is signed.

October 25, 1783   Robert Shurtliff is honorably discharged by the military and cited for heroism.